PRIMED FOR VENGEANCE

GILL D ANDERSON

5-star Readers' Favourite Review

Reviewed by Susan Sewell

A troubled young man targets specific women for murder, and with nothing but a few enigmatic rhymes to follow, the police must stop him before it's too late in the thriller novel Primed For Vengeance by Gill D Anderson. Butch suffered violence and abuse from early childhood, and the only person who gave him any comfort or consideration during his formative years was his neighbor, Kate. After witnessing his father murdering his mother, the authorities place Butch in the Woodlands Residential Care Unit. There Sarah gives him the care and attention that Butch has always needed. However, when Sarah takes a leave of absence shortly before he reaches age and moves from the facility, Butch feels betrayed. Another woman has rejected him: first Kate, and now Sarah. Butch resolves to get even.

Set in the stunning city of Adelaide, Australia, Primed For Vengeance by Gill D Anderson is an unsettling thriller that makes your blood run cold. This disturbing story, shown from multiple points of view, realistically depicts the devastating effects of childhood trauma due to severe abuse. With a heart-rending plot, exciting scenes, and a larger-than-life antagonist, the enthralling story held me captivated from the first page to its shocking conclusion. The antagonist's psychosis has a terrifying realism that is hauntingly memorable. This book will thrill true crime enthusiasts and fans of thrillers who relish a story with actual people woven into a fictional setting. There are some triggers that the author clearly states at the beginning of the book, including violence, murder, and mental health issues, to name a few.

ISBN: 978-1-922578-56-3 (paperback)

Published in Australia by Gill D. Anderson and InHouse Publishing.
www.inhousepublishing.com.au

Printed in Australia by InHouse Print & Design.

IN HOUSE PTY LTD PUBLISHING

NATIONAL LIBRARY OF AUSTRALIA

A catalogue record for this book is available from the National Library of Australia

I would like to warn readers that my novels *Hidden from View, The Chosen Seven, Melita* and *Primed for Vengeance* all have dark themes weaved throughout the storylines. This includes trauma, abuse, violence, murder, sexual deviance and mental health issues. If these themes trigger you in any way, please practice self-care and do not read on.

Primed for Vengeance is purely a work of fiction and in no way represents any children in care or any Australian model of residential care. This novel is based purely on my imagination and experiences of residential care almost two decades ago. It is important to note that South Australia has recently adopted a therapeutic 'sanctuary' care model which is in direct contrast to the fictitious drama depicted in *Primed for Vengeance.*

Dedication

Primed for Vengeance is dedicated to the memory of the late Martin 'Jock' Richardson (loving husband to Kellie, son of Sandy and the late Campbell, and brother to Carol). Jock was a cherished friend to many, a role model to troubled youths, a great colleague and just an all-round legend of a man in general.

To quote my husband Brent, 'Thanks for the memories, mate. I don't think I'll ever meet your like again. You touched so many lives in so many ways. Rest easy, big man. You will be sorely missed.'

The sudden and tragic loss of Jock in October 2020 is still incredibly raw but given that he was so full of love, life and laughter, I will keep this spiel as light-hearted as possible.

Let me start by saying that my intention was to give Jock a tiny wee cameo role in *Primed for Vengeance* but he ended up becoming a hero of sorts! I seriously started to wonder if he was up there laughing and guiding my fingers to type more scenes for him! I can totally imagine him doing this! If so, then you got your own way, Jock!

While the disclaimer correctly states that this story and the characters are a work of fiction, Jock and his family are the exception. With the permission of his wife, mum and sister, I have depicted them exactly as they are (in my eyes).

Jock, I hope you approve!

We love and miss you so much. All my love, from Gill. xxxx

PROLOGUE

March 2021

Butch never used his real name anymore. Nothing was left of him that was remotely like his younger self. Any hope he'd once had was well and truly gone. The ability to give or receive love was never going to become a reality and the likelihood of developing a moral compass or a sense of right or wrong was laughable. To hell with having a conscience! Butch was on a mission. There would be blood, there would be tears and ultimately there would be death. The anticipation of his victim's blood on his hands excited him like nothing else. No other thought made him feel that way, which was unfortunately why there was no choice but to undertake tonight's gruesome task.

His not-so-lucky victim, whom he'd nicknamed 'the heartbreaker', was a regular passenger on the tram. Often she would be sitting close to him without even realising it. The heartbreaker's pretty little face was either buried in her mobile phone like most of the commuters or she would be chatting away to the other regular passengers. Butch knew which stop she would disembark at, given he'd been following her journey to and from work for a while now. The fact that she caught the tram was a blessing because no one thought twice about seeing the same people on the daily commute. Therefore, it would not rouse her suspicion if she were to notice him. As he'd unpacked that thought a little more, a red mist came down over his eyes and he clenched his fists tightly. The realisation that she had *not* in fact noticed his recent presence on the tram suddenly felt like a knife through his heart. Butch squeezed his eyes shut tight, willing himself not to explode. He must try to stay calm while on public transport. In her defence, he'd pulled his hooded top down low, covering his head and face most of the time. So essentially he was using a disguise of sorts. Sometimes he wore wraparound sunglasses too. This was partly to avoid eye contact with others and partly to remain incognito *but still... Shouldn't she know my walk, my mannerisms, and the very essence of me?* Butch began to twitch. This had to be done properly. The plan needed to unfold exactly as envisioned for it to have maximum impact.

Over the last few weeks, Butch managed to tune in to the heartbreaker's conversations with other regular passengers she'd become friendly with. He shook his head in disgust as he thought of how easy it was to find out her short-term plans. The heartbreaker obviously wasn't as smart or as streetwise as he'd once given her credit for.

Tonight is the night! Butch's jaw tightened at the thought. The middle-aged woman sitting next to him gave him a sideways glance, her eyes blinking rapidly. The woman noted the strange young man's breathing was becoming shallow as his eyes darted about the carriage. As the woman sensed his frenzied state and noted the prominent Adam's apple bobbing up and down in his throat she thought to herself: *It looks like it might burst forth from his neck at any moment!* At first, she considered that the young man may be having a seizure or medical episode of sorts, but then her gut instinct told her he was mentally unstable. She promptly decided to move to a vacant seat nearby.

Butch closed his eyes and managed to calm himself using a slow breathing technique that a therapist had taught him many moons ago. There were times when it worked, and other times when it didn't. A minute later his head snapped up and his eyes pinged open. Butch was outraged to see that the bitch who'd been sitting next to him in the carriage was now sitting in the seat in front. *What the hell? Does she think she is too good to sit next to the likes of me?* Butch moved into the vacant seat directly behind the woman so he could lean over and talk into her ear.

'Snobby slut!' he hissed, his breath hot on the back of her neck. The woman froze, immediately full of regret that her move to another seat had offended him. Feeling intimidated, the woman stared straight ahead and didn't react. Meanwhile the effect of his menacing vibe and aggressive tone made her insides turn to liquid. In a bid to become invisible, she slid down into her seat a little. The woman pushed her glasses up her sweaty nose and hoped he couldn't tell she was shaking as her heart thumped painfully in her chest.

Butch was well aware of how he'd made the woman feel. *Look at her trying to shrink, to make herself disappear! I know that feeling only too well!* He loved to intimidate people; in fact, he absolutely thrived on it. After all, it was the only power he had in his life. This put him in control, and he liked that a lot. Butch was contemplating his next move when he realised the tram was pulling in to stop number ten. The heartbreaker would be getting off! It was lucky for the woman who'd pissed him off that he had more pressing things to deal with. *It's party time!* The heartbreaker deserved what was coming to her, no question about that.

As Butch followed his victim from a short distance, he was dismayed to notice that her petite figure was heading towards Bene Bistro, a popular place for after-work drinks. *Why is she doing this instead of taking the usual route in the opposite direction towards the street she lives in?* The heartbreaker always went straight home after work. The exact routine was etched into his head. Why had the dumb bitch chosen to go somewhere different tonight? He didn't have time to make changes to his well-thought-out plan! He hovered for a moment, uncertain of what to do next. If he went to Bene Bistro, he'd have to wait around like a dickhead waiting for her to leave. God only knew how long she might stay there. If she'd gone straight home as usual, she'd have been dead by nightfall. Like many who planned to kill, Butch did not like any changes to the victim's routine. Any deviation caused a level of anxiety about the unknown. Butch swiftly reached the conclusion that he wouldn't follow through with his plan tonight after all. He wasn't jealous about who the heartbreaker might be meeting, because the reality was that soon she would not be meeting anyone ever again.

Highly irritated, Butch turned on his heel to catch the tram back in the opposite direction. When he reached the tram stop, he punched the shelter with such force that his knuckles split open. A young Asian couple scurried away, talking rapidly in their native language, their faces pinched with fear. The man pointed down the street and Butch guessed he said something along the lines of 'let's walk to the next tram stop rather than stand next to the crazy guy'. The woman vigorously nodded her head in agreement. Butch didn't need to understand their words to get the general gist of the conversation. Fear was universal and so was body language. When Butch looked down at his hand which was dripping blood everywhere, he suddenly roared with laughter. Butch found it comical the way the couple overreacted due to their obvious fear of him. His manic laughter made them quicken their pace and he laughed harder still. *Fuck, my emotions are all over the place tonight!*

Only a few seconds after finding the situation hilarious, Butch suddenly felt flat and empty. *I'm not right in the head.* He moodily pulled off his hooded sweater and wrapped one of the arms around his hand to stem the blood flow. He'd read a wanky quote once that stated it is impossible to be angry and laugh at the same time because anger and laughter are mutually exclusive. Butch had tossed the self-help book in the bin with disgust. These self-help gurus were all liars and bastards. He was living proof that you *could* be angry and laugh at the same time. Butch realised he rarely laughed at the same things other people found comical, though. Instead he laughed at people who were afraid. Scaring others was a great release of pent-up tension. *I enjoy being cruel.*

No one else appeared at the tram stop, which suited him fine. Butch was unaware of the other commuters who'd spotted him on the platform, took one look at the blood dripping from his hand and then decided to walk in the opposite direction. His deranged laughter was the deciding factor for one lady who promptly called for an Uber instead.

The raw weeping flesh on his knuckles stung. Butch relished the pain; it was a welcome distraction. Butch used to cut himself a lot during his early teenage years. Now he only self-harmed when he was frustrated about something. The sting of slicing his skin followed by the beautiful sweet release of blood was a relief as the pain helped to distract him from his mental anguish. The shock kept him present and mindful. Cutting himself helped to shift his focus from his early memories. His body was covered in scars, but they suited him. Many were self-inflicted, but a few were inflicted by others. They were ugly just like him. Butch believed he was rotten to the core. As a kid he had often wondered whether maggots would swarm out of him if he were to slit himself open. He was so sure that would be the case. He was bad through and through, like a rotten apple.

Butch often questioned the point of being on this earth. Maybe he was an alien? He honestly did not know who he was and suffered with identity issues due to having no living relatives to compare himself to. He'd written songs to that effect in a previous life and was proud of the haunting lyrics that were so different to the shit songs in the charts these days. Even though he'd only recently left his teen years behind, he was not into the constant crap on the radio. The lyrics were all about booty and hoes; it was pathetic.

Butch's father had recently passed away in prison from a genetic heart condition that Butch had inherited. *Thanks, Dad! Great legacy to leave me!* There were now no relatives left on either the paternal or maternal side of the family. *Boo-hoo, no one cares!*

Butch was still figuring out who he was. During his teenage years, he'd been asked by a guidance teacher in high school what would give him a sense of achievement. The first thing that came to his mind was to kill another, but he did not verbalise this. Butch was initially shocked at the evil thought and tried to push it down and dismiss it somehow. But that was back in the days when he'd still felt a shred of hope. It was during a time when he still might have amounted to something. Now he welcomed the dark evil thoughts when they came.

Not many people could say they'd killed someone. Murder would most definitely be his biggest achievement. The heartbreaker was one of the few people who'd ever made him feel like he mattered and then the bitch had pulled the rug right out from under his feet. She'd made him start to believe he might make it in life, but then she'd made the fatal mistake of abandoning him when he needed her most. Whatever he might have become was gone in an instant without her support. The heartbreaker would pay for this. There was simply no other way for her to redeem herself. Tonight, she'd messed up yet again. *Not to worry; there is always next time.* So it would seem that the heartbreaker would live to see another sunrise after all. Of course she wasn't the *only* heartbreaker who'd featured in his life, but she was the main culprit and therefore the main target. *For now.*

Butch knew the heartbreaker stayed at Port Elliot every Easter and now thanks to her blabbering to all and sundry on the tram, he knew the exact details of her upcoming annual trip right down to the time they'd be setting off on Good Friday. This was a family tradition that had taken place for many years. Oh yes, he knew a lot about her life, way more than was necessary or appropriate. He could not deny he was mildly obsessed with her.

CHAPTER 1

Good Friday 2021

Following the missed opportunity with his original murder plan, Butch waited with bated breath for the long weekend to come around. As predicted, the heartbreaker and her family were headed towards the pretty town situated in the sheltered Horseshoe Bay. At the start of the long weekend, amid the flurry of cars, Butch headed towards the south-east coast of the Fleurieu Peninsula.

Although Butch kept a safe distance, the temptation to speed up and run the heartbreaker's car off the road was huge. He used every ounce of his willpower not to do so. While it would be satisfying, his mission would be over too quickly and there would not be enough gore or suffering for his liking. *Patience, patience, patience!*

Once Butch had taken note of the exact location of the large four-bedroom holiday rental home the heartbreaker would be staying at, he'd completed a U-turn and headed to the famous Port Elliot Bakery. He decided to indulge in a large coffee and an iced doughnut. *It's too early to go in for the kill just yet. All good things come to those that wait.*

The bakery had a nice vibe and was full of friendly smiley staff. Butch inhaled deeply, savouring the wonderful aroma which was a mixture of warm pastry and baking bread. He let out a loud derisive snort as he considered how the locals would not be smiling for much longer when they heard about the brutal murder that was about to occur on their own doorstep.

A young couple who'd been served before Butch glanced his way. They appeared wary as they walked by him with takeaway coffees, their clingy active wear outlining their perfect physiques. Most people would be offended at the way people looked at Butch, but he thrived on it. *Oh, lookie here! Little Ms blondie and her meathead boyfriend think I'm a weirdo – whoop, whoop!* He deliberately muttered his thoughts out loud but was unsure if the couple had made out what he'd said. The blonde girl sporting tight leggings and a cropped top must have heard him, as her head jerked backwards in his direction, her eyes wide and fearful. Butch watched the super-toned girl whisper something to her muscly boyfriend who in turn glanced back at Butch through narrowed eyes. Butch cocked his head to one side and gave his best penetrating stare. The boyfriend unconsciously flexed his biceps in a bid to demonstrate his strength which amused Butch to no end. Despite their show of bravado, the couple decided not to engage with the strange-looking boy. Instead they quickened their pace to put distance between them. Butch bellowed with laughter, which caused more wary glances from other patrons to come his way. *The boyfriend is all muscles but no balls*! Butch thought he might get a hard-on at this rate. Nothing got him off as much as other people's fear. Now the whole place was looking at him! He could burst all their heads open like watermelons right now if he wanted to! *Pop, pop, pop! Imagine the mess of a mass blast like that!*

For the second time that day, Butch resisted temptation; no use in detracting from the main job at hand here. Much to the relief of everyone in the vicinity of the bakery, he clutched his large flat white close to his chest and sauntered down the street towards his borrowed car. A few people watched the tall gothic-looking lanky figure to make sure he was leaving the area. The locals were protective of their little town and weirdos who killed the usual happy vibes were not welcome.

As Butch slid into the driver's seat, he pulled down the rear-view mirror and looked at his goofy gummy grin, his decayed teeth on display. *I'm ugly to the core.* He'd been eligible for free dental care in a former life but had refused point-blank to get his teeth fixed, much to the dismay of the adults who pretended to give a shit. Why would he? Looking ugly was part of his persona. Why did that have to be wrong? The last dentist who'd tried to push his agenda on him had received a nasty bite on the arm. Consequently, Butch was banned from the dental surgery, which suited him fine.

Butch looked down at his filthy nails as he considered exploring the idyllic seaside town nestled between Victor Harbor and Middleton. He eventually decided against it, as he was afraid of becoming side tracked from his mission. He was known to vague out and lose track of time and that would simply not do. The lure was hard to resist due to Port Elliot's postcard-worthy beaches, dramatic coastline and charming streets. He needed to drive to somewhere a bit more secluded, somewhere less enticing. *I've already pissed off a few of the locals; that will have to do for now. Maybe I should have a micro-nap instead.* He decided to conk out on the back seat for a bit. He'd resurrect when it was time.

CHAPTER 2

Two and a half years ago Woodlands Residential Care Unit, Adelaide

Sarah Whitaker was exhausted following a drawn out and somewhat hellish shift at work. She glanced at the time on her laptop display and noted she'd worked almost a double shift despite being rostered to knock off several hours ago. Sarah sighed and stretched her arms high above her head, then rubbed the back of her neck. Her intention was to finish one more case plan and then she'd definitely make a move to go home. The office was eerily quiet when she was the only one in there. So many crazy scenes had taken place right here in this room that she imagined the place would surely be affected by dark energy. Maybe the staff would benefit from burning a stick of sage in each wing. This might get rid of the negative vibrations following the constant physical fights, screaming matches and emotional meltdowns. Some of the residents ended up being restrained for their own safety when their anger overtook them and they became a danger to themselves and others. Sarah shuddered as a few scenes she'd rather not revisit came to mind. Woodlands Residential Care Unit (affectionately referred to as Woodies) was a care option for young people who were unable to live with their parents and ended up in the care of the state government.

The office had a private area for the residents to seek support, vent to staff or discuss any incidents they were involved in. The welcoming space was also where the staff were expected to keep on top of never-ending paperwork relating to each young person in their care. Staff were expected to juggle supervising residents, type up never-ending critical incident report forms and constantly ensure all the case plans were up to date for each young person. This was no mean feat due to the regularity of critical incidents requiring all hands on deck. Sometimes it was worth waiting until all residents were settled down for the night to complete any pressing paperwork.

On top of that, the youth workers were expected to keep the young people engaged in various education programs, take them to appointments and involve them in activities they enjoyed. Keeping on top of all of those things seemed impossible, yet the staff at the unit gave it their all in an attempt to achieve the best outcomes for the residents in their care.

The office reminded Sarah of a goldfish bowl due to the way it was fitted out in a glass semi-circle. The desks faced outwards towards the main communal area of the unit. This created a two-way view for both staff and residents. The staff often joked about how the office was similar to sitting in the cockpit of a plane.

Sarah was hardworking and ambitious. Despite obtaining a Bachelor's degree in social work then going on to undertake further studies in psychology, she'd somehow ended up back working at Woodies. The unit was where she'd undertaken her second university placement. At the time, she'd felt that while she enjoyed the placement, it was unlikely that working in residential care would fully utilise her skill set. Over time, Sarah realised she missed working there and to the delight of the staff, she decided to return at the end of her studies. By returning to Woodies as an employee, Sarah had come full circle, but she would not have it any other way. Her parents were dismayed when she'd returned to work at the unit, believing she was carved out for better things. But they were somewhat appeased when she quickly climbed the ranks and became the unit manager. Sarah was quick to assure her family that while the youth workers did not have degrees, they were a talented group of people who had unique skill sets and a special way with the residents that many qualified people would simply never possess. It took a certain selfless and empathetic type of person to be a successful youth worker. Sarah had observed many allied health professionals interact with the residents and found it interesting that often the more qualified they were, the less they were able to build rapport with the young people.

Sarah offered so much more than counselling and advocacy to the youths she worked with. Sarah was wholly invested in making a genuine positive impact on the residents' lives and became a constant reliable presence for them. It was important to Sarah that the residents felt they could always count on her. This was an admirable trait, but many of her colleagues saw it as her downfall. Some worried that one day Sarah would overstep the boundaries and give too much of herself. So far nothing adverse had happened. After all, the staff were not the parents of these traumatised young people. No matter how good any of them were at their jobs, the team was acutely aware that they could never replace the role of real family members. The young people were not stupid; they knew at the end of the day that the staff were merely doing their job, even if it was one they were passionate about.

The facility consisted of two separate wings, with four bedrooms each. This was to separate the opposite sexes, although these days the kids were showing increasing opposition about which area they belonged in because gender identity was such a prominent theme presently. The residents were encouraged to talk about such things knowing that they would be supported by their caregivers. Sometimes the kids were just being difficult though, so it was a long-standing joke for the residents to say that they didn't know if they were Arthur or Martha, in order to wind the staff up.

The criteria for eligible residents to be admitted to Woodies had changed somewhat over the years. When the unit opened a decade ago, it was strictly for thirteen-to-eighteen-year-olds needing an emergency placement following removal from their parents' care. Due to the lack of foster care placements in recent years, this meant that the children being admitted to Woodies were becoming younger and staying longer. In the past, the teenagers who were accepted into the unit had to have a certain profile and be a 'good fit' with the other residents. The state needed to deem them as suitable to live in a placement that provided routines and predictability. These days, there were children as young as nine years of age being admitted. They would arrive clutching their soft toys, unprepared for the harsh realities of residential care. Although everything was under lock and key, including the bedrooms, the staff did their utmost to make Woodies as homely as possible.

Despite the ongoing efforts of staff to make Woodies cosy and inviting, the state government funding was starting to dry up. This was due to the staff replacing broken windows and damaged furniture once too often. These days, everything looked cheap, from the yellow nylon curtains to the threadbare cushions on the worn sofa. When Sarah first took up part-time shifts at the unit as a university student, she'd done so for her own learning. But when the young woman realised how the place was being run, she quickly became invested in making several positive changes and she'd sneaked in some colourful throws and cushions purchased from a charity shop to brighten the place up a bit.

Sarah was no Mother Teresa, but she was a natural born leader. She possessed a bubbly personality and a way of relating to the kids that even those with many years of experience simply didn't possess. Given that most of the kids responded well to Sarah, she rapidly became a well-respected and valuable manager. Sarah's role was exhausting and often thankless. A lot of the time, she felt little sense of achievement as the kids often appeared ungrateful and aggressive. The staff turnover was high due to the demanding nature of the role and unfortunately this only made the kids even more mistrusting of adults than they already were. They didn't have many constant presences in their life, so it was understandable when they refused to open up. Many of them had been through numerous social workers in the space of a few years, so it was no surprise when they got to the stage where they no longer wanted to engage with anyone in authority.

Sarah glanced up and could see the staff had everything under control. Five of the kids were in the games room with two youth workers and the remaining three residents were watching an approved movie in the lounge with Kerry and Jock, who were highly experienced youth workers. The three kids watching the movie were the ones Sarah worried about the most. Beth Nelson was the angriest girl she'd ever worked with and a few of the dark stories she'd written could be used as horror movie material. Beth sometimes went as far as smearing her own blood on her handiwork. Despite the constant checks for contrabands, somehow the kids would still sneak them into the unit. Beth often managed to get her hands on sharp objects to vandalise either her room or cut her body with. The residents were inventive; there was no doubt about that. *Who knew that the plastic clip on a loaf of bread could do so much damage when broken in half?* The unit cook was suitably upset when she realised she'd carelessly left the innocent-looking bit of plastic lying out on the kitchen bench.

Beth was known to snap easily, her vicious temper often resulting in the unit being locked down and the police being called. Beth had experienced horrendous neglect and emotional abuse before being removed from her mother's care. The sour-faced girl refused to attend therapy and instead lashed out at others at every opportunity.

Only a month ago, Beth had escalated at the dinner table and stabbed Skye, her least favourite resident, in the eye with a fork – all because she'd thought the other girl was looking her up and down in a 'judgy way'. Pandemonium had ensued with Beth being restrained, Skye being whisked off to hospital in an ambulance and the police taking statements from everyone present. Despite staff providing close supervision, these incidents still occurred at times because they were often completely out of the blue. There was no rhyme or reason to the residents' behaviours. They were young people who were simply not wired the same way as those who'd been raised by protective and loving parents. Sadly, the staff were not always privy to the triggers that set the residents off. Therefore it was difficult to assess what might be causing these outbursts or to develop a heightened awareness towards them.

The paperwork for such incidents was never-ending and only detracted from finding time to comfort and support the other residents. Thankfully Beth had only superficially scratched Skye's eye and she would recover without having her eyesight affected. Skye refused to press charges and once again Beth got away with her increasingly violent behaviour. Skye was moved to another residential care placement at her request but unfortunately Beth remained at Woodies and continued her unpredictable and violent behaviour, which was a constant worry for staff who always felt that they were walking on eggshells around her.

Beth was close to transitioning into independent living accommodation but would still need significant support, post care. The thing that shocked Sarah the most was the fact that once Beth had calmed down, she showed no remorse whatsoever. Beth merely shrugged when she was advised her actions could have blinded Skye.

'I don't fuckin' care; the bitch deserved it!' she drawled, her black beady eyes glittering in her chalk-white face.

Sarah knew this wasn't bravado talking; she could tell Beth meant every word and it chilled her to the bone. Beth's psychological profile indicated that she exhibited the characteristics of antisocial personality disorder, which was typified by the pervasive disregard of the rights and feelings of others. Sarah made a mental note to make Beth's exit plan a priority for discussion at the next team meeting. Somehow, she couldn't envisage Beth leaving care without leaving some sort of unwanted parting gift to the residential care home she openly despised.

Sarah took a sip of cold tea and glanced up at the sound of laughter from the lounge area. She smiled because it wasn't something she heard often enough around the place. Sarah discreetly observed the three kids glued to the *School of Rock* movie. They were caught up in the moment, lost in the crazy humorous antics of the main actor, Jack Black. The cosy scene warmed Sarah's heart, yet it made her incredibly sad at the same time.

Corey Logan was giggling incessantly at a scene where Jack Black was encouraging a group of school kids to break all the rules while in class. Sarah smiled. It was so lovely to see his face light up and his eyes shine; this was truly a rare sight. Corey was acting like the carefree boy that he should be. Yet if he knew he was being watched, he would quickly display his usual surly 'tough guy' persona that the other kids were used to seeing. Corey required extra monitoring because he was sneakier in his abuse of the other residents than the openly aggressive ones. Being the youngest and most angelic looking, it was easy to forget how manipulative he could be. He'd managed to get other kids to shoplift for him during outings and told compulsive lies to cause a rift between those that got on well. It was draining to try and manage because without having one-on-one staff, a lot of his behaviour would slip by unnoticed.

In an ideal world, Corey would never have been placed at Woodies, but the reality was, there simply had been no other placement options available when he was removed from his parents' care. Sarah recalled the day he had arrived at the unit with his meagre belongings, clutching a small brown teddy bear. He was nine years old with huge blue eyes and a mop of golden hair. The poor kid looked petrified, given that the other residents were in their mid- to late teens and clearly significantly more advanced and streetwise than him.

Corey quickly morphed into one of the gang, mimicking the behaviours and attitudes of his older peers to fit in. Sarah tried her best to separate him from the others so he could take part in more age-appropriate activities. Corey loved this at first but quickly realised how childish he seemed next to the others. Sarah found it heartbreaking because she knew how much he secretly treasured their outings to the local bowling alley and trips to the cinema to watch Disney movies. The only thing Sarah managed to maintain was reading *Harry Potter* novels to him at bedtime. Having secret one-on-one time was the only way to engage Corey in something he truly enjoyed without the others knowing about it.

Sarah treasured those moments; this was when the real Corey would emerge. He was bright, inquisitive and eager to become lost in the magical world of Hogwarts. She would read to him until his eyes glazed over and he drifted off to sleep. One Christmas, Sarah gave Corey a wizard hat and wand. This was kept secret from the others and therefore they were stashed away in his chest of drawers, away from prying eyes. They only came out at bedtime when no one else was around. Those days were gone now, and the blond curls were replaced with a severe crew cut and a permanent scowl.

Sarah's gaze turned to Shaun Wallace; he was the resident who'd resided at Woodies the longest. There weren't any foster carers willing to take him on, due to his extreme behaviours. He was watching the movie, but his face was hard to read. Shaun adopted his usual blank expression. The staff often referred to his look as 'the lights are on, but nobody is home'. Being able to tell when Shaun was present was difficult. He remained in a persistent vague state, with a faraway look in his eyes. Often his responses were automatic, his mind clearly somewhere else. The other kids were intimidated by Shaun. Unlike them, he didn't have to bully, manipulate or physically attack his peers to scare them. He simply gave them a penetrating look with his dark grey soulless eyes, and they were quaking in their boots.

The staff were painfully aware that their rotating shifts added to the instability for the kids and understood it was far from an ideal parenting model. However, at present, there were no better alternatives on offer. As a department, the staff felt assured they were doing the best with what was available to them. It was widely acknowledged that the issues they faced were systemic, rather than due to poor management. State care was something the general public failed to understand. At times, Sarah's friends and family criticised the care model the unit offered and questioned how she could work in such an environment. Sarah would boldly look them in the eye and ask them what the alternatives were; whether they could come up with any bright ideas, or better still, were they willing to become a foster carer for any of the residents themselves? That usually shut them right up. Sarah had zero tolerance for armchair experts and ignorant people who were quite happy to criticise the residential care model yet offered no better solutions. If there were an abundance of foster carers, then there would be no place for residential care homes; however, there weren't, so those that were opposed to them provided a pointless argument.

Sarah found it impossible to get away from the fact that while the physical needs of the kids at Woodies were met, it was very difficult to give them the love and nurture they so badly needed. Staff were only allowed to display a limited amount of affection due to rules and regulations to limit the likelihood of allegations of inappropriate touching being made.

Sarah thought back to poor Keith, who'd been a lovely youth worker and a great mentor for the kids. He'd made the fatal mistake of allowing Isabella, a twelve-year-old girl to hug him whenever she asked. He'd genuinely felt sorry for her and was trying to be a father figure by offering comfort and affection. But this went from innocent hugs to Isabella wanting to sit on Keith's lap while watching movies. He was not comfortable with this and explained the need for personal space and boundaries. Being the extremely insecure young girl that she was, Isabella had taken his rejection personally and became revengeful and spiteful. When Keith began engaging with the other residents instead of Isabella as an avoidance tactic, she'd turned nasty and told a teacher at school that Keith was inappropriately touching her. He was immediately suspended from work and hauled over the coals while an investigation took place. Isabella played the victim role to a tee and had everyone fooled except the staff at Woodies, who knew they'd been vigilant in ensuring Keith was never alone with her. In the end, the allegations were not substantiated but Keith was moved to another unit to put distance between him and Isabella.

The other kids were outraged and furious with Isabella. The allegations against Keith were meant to remain highly confidential, but she'd bragged about the incident to anyone who would listen while boldly pointing at the *Charter of Rights for Children and Young People in Care* poster displayed outside the staff office. The other kids were sad about losing Keith; he'd displayed boundless energy and was full of ideas for new fun activities and games they could play. The staff found it difficult not to judge Isabella and continue to treat her equally because the general sense of injustice was palpable.

Even Sarah, who was usually so forgiving, struggled at the girl's lack of concern in relation to the impact of her behaviour on the other residents and on Keith's career. The truth was that Isabella craved attention and enjoyed the power and control that the whole situation gave her. Sarah reflected that, unfortunately, sometimes the most damaged kids were so damn unlikable, not to mention dangerous. That was the ugly truth, but Sarah would never give up looking for the good in them and this was why the kids at Woodies simply adored her. During times like these, Sarah tried to take her own emotions out of the equation and remember her training. She often used a line one of her lecturers had quoted at university: *If we can change our thinking from 'a child is seeking attention' to 'they are seeking connection', this changes everything. We as practitioners can then view the behaviour and its meaning in a completely different context.*

CHAPTER 3

Sarah's mind wandered back to her first-ever shift at Woodies many moons ago. The whole unit was getting ready to go on an excursion to the local markets. Such excursions were fun for the kids but were often draining for the staff. Out in public, the residents were much harder to keep in order when they decided to misbehave. As such, the outings were all planned with military precision to ensure the safety of the kids and the public.

Sarah recalled being utterly shocked when the staff explained that Shaun would have to stay back at the unit as he wasn't allowed to join them on outings anymore. His social worker was coming over to play table tennis with him instead. Sarah frowned disapprovingly.

'Isn't that non-inclusive leaving him behind? It must be so sad for him to know he is the only one not going.'

The staff exchanged knowing looks indicating a secret code for 'she's new to this; she doesn't get it.' Larry, who was the manager at the time, picked up a manila folder and handed it to Sarah thinking that while she was smart, she still had a lot to learn.

Larry shrugged his jacket on while addressing Sarah.

'I tell you what, why don't you stay behind with Shaun and his social worker; she'd probably appreciate the support. Read his file and you will get the picture about why he can't come with us.'

Sarah was torn; she'd been keen to go on the outing with the others, but her curiosity got the better of her.

'Okay' she nodded, unsure if her earlier comments had got her on the wrong foot with Larry. Once everyone had departed, she tried to engage with Shaun and his social worker, but they seemed content with just the two of them playing table tennis, so she returned to the office and opened the manila file containing Shaun's psychological assessment.

Sarah's heart constricted as she read about Shaun's early years. His parents had emotionally and physically abused him regularly during his formative years. A hospital report was stuffed in the back section of the file. Sarah found a paediatrician's report that described how Shaun reportedly 'fell down a flight of stairs' when he was four years old. His parents' explanation of his injuries was inconsistent, and the treating doctor suspected he'd been thrown down the stairs. The medical report further indicated that Shaun was clearly hesitant about telling his version of events and was inconsistent in his recount. The nature of the injuries was assessed by the examining doctor as likely to be non-accidental; however, not enough evidence was gathered due to the lack of a disclosure to substantiate physical abuse and therefore, he was allowed to return home.

Sarah was moved to tears when she came to the part in Shaun's case notes about the young woman living next door who had made several reports about her concerns to the Child Abuse Report Line. She'd overheard Shaun's mother telling him he was 'a useless piece of shit' on a regular basis. The woman could often be heard verbally abusing her young son in the street. The neighbour also reported that Shaun was often left home alone to fend for himself while his parents gambled away their welfare payments or went on lengthy drinking sessions at the local pub. The Department for Child Protection had clearly undertaken the necessary welfare checks; however, Shaun's parents were clever at manipulating the system. The young couple ensured no concerns were found when social workers did random visits to the home. It was frustrating that no actions could be undertaken with nil evidence of any abuse. The social workers' hands were tied due to no fault of their own.

Later accounts from Shaun during therapy indicated that his parents often beat each other up. He became adept at managing this by hiding in his wardrobe with his hands over his ears until they stopped. The authorities remained aware of the family, but unfortunately, whenever police were called, there just so happened to be nothing to charge them with when they investigated. The picture being built up of the family was still hearsay. No arrests or child removals could occur without evidence or clear substantiation of domestic violence or child abuse. Shaun's parents were extremely clever and knew how the system worked, both having grown up in families who were adept at avoiding the police and welfare agencies.

Sarah surmised that this was where the system had let Shaun down because anyone in authority visiting that house would have an inkling of what was going on. Proving it in order to take action was an entirely different matter, however. The situation was so frustrating for the diligent workers who truly wanted to help make a difference. So poor Shaun suffered all kinds of abuse day and night and no one was ever there at the right time to catch his parents red-handed and intervene. Sarah wiped the tears from her eyes as she willed herself to keep reading.

The next section of the file outlined Shaun's account to the child psychologist about the night that changed his life forever. Sarah steadied herself and took a deep breath as she read on.

A few days before his seventh birthday, Shaun had woken up in the middle of the night due to his parents screaming vicious insults at each other. Nothing was unusual about that, so he had curled up in the foetal position and put his hands over his ears like he always did. But this fight was different. His mum was screaming for help and a lot of banging and crashing was going on. Shaun described that he'd felt wobbly and jelly-like. The hairs had stood up on the back of his neck.

He'd slipped out of bed and tiptoed down the narrow hallway towards the small kitchenette where his parents were throwing crockery at each other. His mother's black bushy hair and wild kohl-rimmed eyes had reminded Shaun of a Halloween witch as she'd pranced around throwing anything she could get her hands on at her husband.

Shaun had described his dad as a boxer due to his short stocky frame and shiny bald head. Shaun said his dad had danced around his mum while waving around a broken beer glass. Shaun told the psychologist that he'd watched his parents fight but just stood there and didn't move. The scene before him was scary but from what the psychologist had gathered, the boy had become accustomed to the regular drama. Shaun described how he had noticed the broken glass and crockery all over the ceramic floor tiles. His dad's foot was badly cut and Shaun recalled wondering if he knew it was bleeding. Shaun said he'd opened his mouth to tell his dad about the cut but then closed it again. The little boy knew something was different about this fight; he could feel it. His dad was going to kill his mum. Shaun was able to articulate to the psychologist that he could sense it somehow. He'd no sooner had the thought when his dad plunged the broken glass straight into his mum's jugular vein just above her collarbone. Shaun was unable to describe the scene in great detail, but as he grew older, he confided to his therapist that he experienced frequent debilitating vivid flashbacks of his mum choking and spluttering, with blood bubbling from her mouth and throat. Shaun was later able to describe the look of shock on his mum's face as she died.

Shaun began to suffer with graphic nightmares about blood pouring from his mum's neck. A specific memory of an image began to play on a constant loop: Shaun kept dreaming about his mum's head lolling to one side and his dad repeatedly screaming, 'What have I done?' The memories flooded his subconscious of his mum making strange gurgling noises followed by a deathly silence. Shaun described how he had stood there frozen like a statue while his father sobbed and called the police, to turn himself in. Sometimes when Shaun tried to sleep, this scenario played on repeat. Insomnia became his friend. As he grew older, writing poems and songs became his only way to escape.

Sarah recalled vividly how she'd clapped a hand over her mouth in horror and shut Shaun's file for a few seconds as if to distance herself from what she'd just read. She'd thought it was enough to digest for one day and that she probably shouldn't read anymore due to the feeling it gave her in the pit of her stomach. She'd found that the packed lunch she'd been looking forward to devouring was suddenly unappealing, after reading such a gruesome family history. The theory lessons at university were one thing; however, the practice of dealing with real live human beings was awful for an empathetic person like her. Sarah tried to busy herself with other tasks at the unit, but then it suddenly occurred to her that she was yet to reach the part in the case file that explained why Shaun was not permitted to go on outings with the other residents. Feeling intrigued, she reluctantly opened his file again to get the missing piece of the puzzle.

Sarah grimaced as she read on to find out that Shaun's father had been incarcerated for life, following the murder of his wife. As much is it was only justice, she imagined how unbearable it would have been for Shaun losing both parents at once. They may have been highly dysfunctional and abusive, but they were his parents all the same. Shaun was initially placed with his paternal aunt Sheila who had undiagnosed mental health issues and multiple split personalities. Shaun was never able to figure out who she might present as, on any given day. There were days when Sheila was alert and did nice things like take him to the zoo. Other days, she treated him like an animal and made him eat from a dog bowl and walk on all fours.

Shaun was saved a few weeks later by a school attendance counsellor who paid Sheila a visit, seeking an explanation as to why her nephew was rarely at school. The counsellor noticed several red flags and made a report to the Child Abuse Report Line about the way Shaun presented. When child protection workers paid Sheila a visit the following week, the crazed-looking woman announced that she wanted to relinquish Shaun's care because he'd begun killing and dissecting small animals and she was finding bits of their bodies in his room.

Sheila was not so much disturbed by this; she was more annoyed at the mess he was making. This was yet another red flag to the social worker who asked Shaun why he'd killed the animals. He shrugged and replied nonchalantly, 'I want them to feel pain like I do.' When his bedroom was examined, the social worker found various dissected animal carcasses, including a dead pigeon with its legs hacked off and its eyes scratched out. Shaun explained he did such things when he was home alone in the garden and felt bored. Sheila was adamant he should leave her care, which was convenient as she was no longer deemed a suitable caregiver.

Upon examining the kinship assessment report, it appeared that Sheila had passed the original assessment with flying colours due to presenting as one of her respectable split personalities at the time. Sheila was later found to be in cahoots with an unethical doctor who'd omitted her mental health history from her medical report. Thus it was never flagged as an issue during the social worker's assessments. This particular doctor was later struck off for taking part in several similar dodgy deals with other patients.

When Sheila presented as her alter ego named Mabel, she was a high-functioning intelligent woman. When she was Sheila, she was a loose cannon. Personality disorders ran in the family and the various professionals involved in Shaun's care team intended to monitor him for any early signs as he grew older. But because Shaun was so insular, it would prove difficult to gauge.

The only suitable placement available for Shaun at the time was Woodlands Residential Care Unit. Sheila took her own life only days after Shaun left her care and the true extent of her abuse of Shaun was never fully uncovered. Given his extensive trauma background, his behaviour was closely monitored upon his admission to the unit and several assessments were undertaken by various healthcare professionals.

Sarah became impatient as she read on; the file was so thick, she thought she'd never get to the part she was looking for. Most files were now electronic but given that this file was so big, no one had got around to converting it yet. The file conversion was on the ever-growing to-do list. Sarah flicked through the pages, hoping to come across the reason Shaun was not allowed to go on unit outings. She stopped as she came across a part B for the case file. *There it is!*

It transpired that during an outing with Woodies residents and staff at a local shopping centre, Shaun had managed to break away from the group who were out with two youth workers named Simon and Joe. The staff had made the fatal mistake of minimising the concerns about Shaun's previous abuse of animals and had taken their eyes off him briefly. Consequently, Shaun had targeted a two-year-old girl whose mum was busy chatting to someone she'd bumped into and was momentarily distracted. Shaun saw an opportunity and grabbed the toddler by the arm, almost yanking it out of its socket. By the time everyone had become attuned to the screams of the child, Shaun had sunk his teeth into the girl's lower arm and bitten so hard it was almost through to the bone. It was a savage attack, one that witnesses compared to being attacked by a Rottweiler, given Shaun's reluctance to release his teeth and let go. Both the girl and her mother screamed hysterically while a sea of witnesses swarmed around the scene trying to separate the children until the emergency services arrived.

As the mayhem unfolded, the more senior of the two youth workers had vomited in his mouth a little. Simon had an inkling he would be suspended from his short-lived employment at Woodies while his questionable supervision of Shaun was investigated.

The child was whisked off to hospital with her sobbing mother who threatened to sue the state and Shaun was promptly referred to Doctor Peter Barnes, the top child psychologist in the state. After a few intensive sessions, Doctor Barnes classified Shaun as displaying the early tendencies of a psychopath who was driven to harm others. The general consensus was that this was a big call to make about a little boy. However, the staff at Woodies were advised to follow Doctor Barnes's recommendation that Shaun not be taken on further outings where one-on-one supervision was not possible. This was due to his assessment that Shaun was a liability and a danger to himself and others while in public.

Doctor Barnes advised Shaun's social worker in a grave tone that he believed the boy presented with all the markings and psychological profiling of a serial killer. Much debate occurred between various mental health professionals about Doctor Barnes's views, which seemed quite extreme, when describing a young developing child. Yet at the same time, no one wanted to be held responsible for reversing the decision for Shaun to remain under strict supervision in case it was career suicide.

As Sarah's thoughts returned to the present she sighed and gave a small shudder. These assessments had been made many years ago. Shaun Wallace was now close to adulthood and would soon be free from the confines of Woodies. Sarah was concerned that Shaun's medical records indicated he'd been born with structural abnormalities of the heart. He required regular medical tests which she was sure he would not follow through with, once he left care. His father had died from the condition while incarcerated so she could only hope Shaun would continue to monitor his condition once he gained independence.

Despite the myriad of post-care services that would be on offer to Shaun, Sarah felt little comfort knowing that he would soon be free to roam wherever he pleased, following his eighteenth birthday.

It would be impossible to enforce any supervision once he left Woodies. The care team couldn't justify flagging him as a risk to the public anymore, particularly as no further major incidents had been reported following the shopping centre incident all those years ago. Sarah's conscience prickled a little and she pushed the thought aside. *He hasn't been involved in any other incidents because we watch him like a hawk at Woodies and don't let him go on group outings. What is he capable of doing, once he is free?*

Sarah realised there was little choice but to give Shaun the benefit of the doubt. In her heart, she truly believed that somehow his time in care had rehabilitated his earlier savage behaviours to a degree. Maybe she also felt a little smug that she'd never felt threatened by him at all. Sure, she'd split up fights he'd been in and mediated following arguments with other residents, but he'd never tried to hurt her physically or mentally like many of the others had. Sarah remembered a catchphrase from a training session she'd attended: *Hurt people hurt people.* For the most part, Shaun Wallace showed Sarah respect and she knew he enjoyed his one-on-one sessions with her immensely, even though he presented with a constant flat affect. *Maybe Shaun is more resilient than we are giving him credit for. I'm going to think positively about his future. After all, we have no control over how he chooses to live, moving forward.*

CHAPTER 4

Despite all the qualifications and credentials held by the staff at Woodies, none of them ever truly understood what their presence meant to the residents. Unless you'd experienced abuse, trauma and neglect, one could never fully grasp the importance of having consistent role models in your life. The kids yearned for someone to offer support and advice to make them feel that their existence mattered. The residents needed adults who would show up every day, say what they meant and mean what they said. There were no mixed messages from the adults at Woodies. If the kids were promised something, then it would absolutely happen. This was an alien concept for most of the residents because their early years had been so unpredictable. The young people took a bit of time getting used to the consistency, but once they did, they thrived on it. Sarah had the reputation as a manager who ran a tight ship. She ensured that the kids experienced equal opportunities to education, connection to kin and the chance to learn independent living skills. Sarah tried to make time for one-on-one sessions with them all as much as possible. Even if it was just taking them for an ice cream on the beach, it was a special time for each resident to be singled out and feel like they mattered.

Most of the kids went to respite care placements at the weekends and could stay with relatives or family friends, provided they were deemed suitable caregivers. It was often the case that there were child protection concerns for these people which prevented them from becoming full-time carers. However they could offer respite, provided an approved person gave discreet supervision during the contact. In the cases where supervision was not required, it was often the case that these relatives had the capacity to provide care but simply did not want to, due to the extreme behaviours of the child. These were the ones that made Sarah's heart ache because she'd observe the kids getting excited about going to stay with relatives for the weekend, but when they were handed back over to Woodies, the kids would inevitably be hurt and feel rejected all over again. They'd often act out because they couldn't understand why they were so unlovable that they could only stay with their relatives for the weekend. It was a catch-22 situation.

The worst-case scenario was when most of the kids were away at the weekend and staff were left with one or two stragglers who did not have anyone coming to pick them up. Such situations were tragic. The staff tended to overcompensate by taking the kids for pizza or to watch a movie, or perhaps take them somewhere they'd always wanted to go. But their smiles never reached their eyes; nothing touched their souls the way that a good old-fashioned dose of love would. Sarah saw the merit in maintaining family contact, but she and her staff were the ones constantly picking up the pieces as a result. Often, a Sunday night was fraught with bad tempers and meltdowns, partly due to kids having to return to the unit after family contact and partly because most of them were not keen to attend their education programs the following day.

Sarah wrote weekly notes in the residents' files so she could monitor where they might be improving or declining in certain areas. She ensured she covered all domains to include their physical, intellectual, emotional and social needs. She noted that Corey was increasingly heartbroken when his grandma brought him back on a Sunday night. The drill was always the same. He'd be full of bravado saying goodbye to his grandma, refusing her kiss or the ruffle of his short, spikey hair with her gnarly hands. But as soon as she left Woodies' premises, his face would crumple, then he'd quickly compose himself, setting his face in his trademark scowl. The scenario was devastating to watch. Sarah always stayed way past her shift on those occasions so that she could spend one-on-one time with Corey at bedtime to read to him.

Corey eventually opened up to Sarah and admitted he felt rejected and couldn't understand why his grandma couldn't care for him full time. He loved going to her place. He'd watch cartoons, drink Ribena and have chocolate biscuits whenever he wanted. Corey described his trips to his grandma as though it were his idea of heaven. The situation tugged at Sarah's heartstrings. Sarah knew that Corey's social worker had approached Corey's grandma about the possibility of her taking on his care full time with supports in place, but she'd declined due to a number of health issues and the fear that her grandson would end up just like his father, Brian, who was her son.

Brian had ended up taking drugs and entering a life of crime. The situation was worsened by the fact that Corey's physical resemblance to his father subconsciously made his grandma believe that history would repeat itself. Corey's grandma made the assumption that Corey was a 'mini-me' replica of his father. Sarah found the familial patterns interesting. Corey's grandma failed to note that her son and grandson were carbon copies of her deceased husband. *Go figure!* Corey's grandma was self-righteous about the fact that she should not have to take on the care of her no-good grandson. Ironically, she failed to see that she'd played a part in the issues experienced by her family. By sweeping things under the carpet when it came to the behaviour her husband had provided as a role model to her son and consequently her grandson, she'd turned a blind eye and become an enabler. No wonder the other males in the family had followed suit! Family histories fascinated Sarah to no end. But she wasn't there to judge; she was there to try and make these kids' lives a little more bearable.

Sarah noted that Shaun's respite care visits were somewhat sporadic over the years too. The young woman who'd reported her concerns to the Child Abuse Report Line when she had lived next door to Shaun and his parents had often looked out for Shaun when he was little. She'd spent a lot of time with him in the garden when he was home alone. Given that Shaun had built up a relationship of sorts with this neighbour during his formative years, his social worker supported him in maintaining contact with her if he so wished. The regularity of the contact varied. Sometimes she'd ask to take him at the weekend, but then she'd claim she was travelling in a mate's camper van for long periods and would fall off the radar again. As Shaun was so difficult to engage and refused to talk openly about his feelings or attend therapy anymore, it was difficult to assess whether he was affected by the reduction in his contact with his old neighbour or not. Sarah got the sense that he wasn't overly fussy about seeing her and felt he only saw her out of obligation. Therefore, she didn't worry too much. Usually the kids were pretty vocal if they did not want to see someone and would simply refuse point-blank to go. Sarah could only surmise that if Shaun continued his occasional outings when the neighbour offered them then he must be fine with the lack of frequency.

Sarah's husband was worried about how consumed she'd become with the young people she worked with. She never seemed to switch off and spent a lot of their leisure time talking about the residents like an old mother hen. One evening after Sarah came home to yet another cold dinner coagulating on the kitchen benchtop, Nick stared at her pointedly.

'You know, Sarah, I do sometimes wonder if you will ever have room in your heart to raise a child of your own since you seem to invest all your time in the kids at Woodies!'

Sarah spun around to face him, reeling from her husband's unexpected attack.

'What the hell? Are you serious? That comment came out of left field a bit, did it not? Is that what you really think? Of course I would be invested in my own child! Maybe I'm so obsessed with the kids at work because you've never given me the vibe that you want us to have our own children!'

Nick was incredulous. 'Are you for real? I've always been too scared to mention trying for a baby, because I feel you won't be able to walk away from Woodies for long enough to focus on your own child!'

Sarah stared back at Nick. 'I can't believe our communication has become poor enough for you to think this! I got the sense it was *you* who wasn't fussy about us having children! Look at how often you are away with work! I hardly think you'd be invested yourself with your current lifestyle! What makes you think that I can't be there for my own child as well as the kids at Woodies? Most mothers work these days, you know!'

Nick looked at Sarah thoughtfully. 'Sometimes, I think you need to take a step back and see things from my perspective. I'm on the outside looking in and can tell you right now that going through a pregnancy when working with the most vulnerable and psychotic teenagers in the state is not going to be the same as going through it in any other regular job. You will be vulnerable and at risk. How often do you have to intervene and restrain kids who are fighting? Not to mention the fact that the kids will be jealous as all hell when they notice your bump growing. They aren't going to like it! You need to think about the bigger picture and what it might mean if we start a family if you are to stay in that job.' Nick stared at his wife imploringly.

Sarah was silent as she digested his words, inwardly acknowledging that his concerns raised valid points. But she was willing to take a chance because she wanted to continue doing the job she loved and now that she knew her husband did want a child, there was no reason why she couldn't do both. She'd take precautions and start maternity leave earlier than most women did.

Sarah calmed down, her feelings of euphoria that Nick wanted to try for a baby overcoming her annoyance at what she saw as an old-fashioned viewpoint. She maintained an optimistic 'where there is a will, there is a way' take on life and she was sure a solution would present itself to make it work. She flopped down next to Nick on the sofa and buried her face into his neck.

'Sorry if I'm a bit fired up; I was just taken aback at how this conversation came about. How about we both look at tweaking our careers to suit parenthood if you manage to knock me up? You'd have to not be away so much too. We both need to consider becoming a bit more family-friendly don't you think?'

Nick's frown softened and he put his arm around Sarah's shoulders. 'What a pair we are, hey? Just goes to show our communication skills need polishing, given we both thought the other wasn't ready to start trying for a baby!' He suddenly sat up straight, his eyes shining. 'Let's start practicing right away! What do you reckon?'

Sarah smiled and cocked her head coquettishly to one side. 'I'm definitely keen!' she grinned. 'We need to think about how we'd balance work and kids but as it might take a while to get pregnant, we'd better get going! I can stop taking the pill straightaway!'

As Nick became carried away in the moment, he scooped up his wife and carried her to the bedroom. He deposited her on the bed and frantically began pulling her dress over her head in a bid to get down to business. *Carpe diem! There's no time like the present.*

CHAPTER 5

Much to Sarah's delight, she became pregnant after only a couple of attempts. The newlyweds had been convinced that it would take a long time. So, while they were pleasantly surprised, they also felt a little unprepared. Sarah tried to keep it quiet for as long as possible, only telling her family and closest friends about the pregnancy. She decided to keep her news from the staff at Woodies initially. Nick became increasingly anxious about Sarah working in such a volatile environment while carrying their precious child, but Sarah kept reassuring him that she knew what she was doing. She promised to work shorter shifts and avoid becoming involved in any of the dramas at work, but she knew it would be no mean feat, given that she'd always been so hands-on.

As Sarah arrived to start the afternoon shift, she quickly scanned the logbook for any major dramas she needed to be aware of. Normally the day team would hand over to the afternoon team with a rundown of what had been happening and would pass on any concerns about the residents. However the morning team were late in returning from a group outing.

Jock burst into the office, his vibrant energy instantly transforming the atmosphere into a jovial space. Sarah smiled; it was impossible not to, when Jock was around. He was secretly her favourite staff member. Jock maintained a great rapport with the young people who all clamoured to hang out with him, given his tendency to be the Woodies comedian and thus the most popular male youth worker.

His real name was Martin but he'd accepted the nickname 'Jock' as he knew the Australians were fond of using this name for Scotsmen. As well as being a clown, Jock also displayed a deep side. Sarah knew he'd undertaken amazing therapeutic work while working one-on-one with the most traumatised residents. He was renowned for his fun camping trips so there were constant requests from the residents to plan the next one.

Jock was from a village called Newcastleton in the Scottish Borders and spoke with a broad accent, often using old Scots dialect that no one had heard of, much to his colleagues' amusement. Instead of learning the local lingo, Jock insisted on everyone learning Scottish slang and it brought much hilarity to everyone around him. The other youth workers were in awe of his magnetic personality and most would agree he was impossible not to gravitate towards. If he wasn't making people laugh, then he was regaling them with a song or two. Whenever they went on a team night out, Jock would always steal the show by amusing them with one of his performances. He was a born entertainer and found it easy to keep any audience in the palm of his hand.

'Now then, ma love,' Jock grinned, 'chuck the kettle oan and lets hae a wee cuppa tea and a blether.'

Sarah welcomed the break from the mound of paperwork on her desk. She stretched her arms upwards and yawned before rising to walk over to the small area designated for staff to make refreshments.

As Sarah pottered around making tea for them both, she glanced over her shoulder to make sure Jock wasn't about to trick her by sneaking up behind her to scare her with a fake rubber insect or snake. He was known to do such things.

Keeping an eye on him as she poured milk into their mugs, Sarah asked, 'What did you get up to on your days off, then, Jock?'

Jock gave her one of his cheeky grins. 'Och ye really dinnae want tae ken, hen!' He gave a low chuckle.

Sarah handed him his special mug with the Rangers football club logo on it. 'Aw come on, Jock, we all know there is never a dull moment with you around. Spill the beans!'

Jock looked amused. 'Well, I went tae a barbeque, which you Aussies do bloody well, by the way... but the mate whae invited me took the piss oot o my tiny wee esky with ma three sausages in it! How wis I meant tae ken that ye are expected tae bring a giant cooler box wae half the bloody butcher and bottle shop in it?' Jock shrugged, an indignant smirk lighting up his handsome features.

Sarah burst into peals of high-pitched laughter, causing Jock to cover his ears and wince. 'Jings woman, dae ye need tae shriek like that?'

'Trust you,' Sarah gasped, wiping away her tears of mirth. 'Where was Kellie? Surely with your wife being an Aussie, she would keep you right on our cultural norms? Ha ha!'

Jock plonked himself into a chair and sipped his tea. 'Kellie was working over the weekend, so I didnae run it past her; rookie error oan my part, eh?'

Sarah giggled and shook her head in mock exasperation. Jock gave an exaggerated sigh and rolled his eyes playfully. He then got to work by scanning the logbook for any critical incidents he was not up to speed with. It was an ingrained habit. Feeling relieved that he didn't spot any for once, he glanced over at Sarah whose earlier smile was replaced with a frown.

'Okay, back to business, Jock. I'm pretty concerned about most of the kids at Woodies for various reasons; it's not often we have so many high-profile kids at the unit at once. I just get the sense that something is going to go down and my hunches are often correct. Is it a full moon or something?'

Switching back into work mode after enjoying the banter, Jock scratched his chin thoughtfully and nodded. 'Yeah, ah ken whit ye mean; the energy is a bit dark around here at the moment. Ah git the feeling something might be aboot tae go doon tae.'

They were interrupted by a commotion outside the office door. With lightning speed Jock and Sarah leapt up simultaneously, nodding at each other to acknowledge that their sixth sense was accurate, as usual. As they entered the communal lounge area, they noted their colleague Kerry was struggling to contain a screaming match between Shaun and Beth, who'd both been in foul moods all day. They were circling each other like a pair of enraged wild animals, each trying to gain the upper hand, both craving the recognition as 'top dog' at Woodies. Sarah straightened up and squared her shoulders as she marched towards the unfolding drama. She used her best authoritative tone.

'What's going on here, guys?' Sarah's eyebrows shot up in a questioning arch.

Beth turned to face Sarah, the venom evident in her expression. 'Dumb prick stole my smokes!' The fierce-looking girl spat out her words, her dark eyes glittering as she bobbed around with her fists clenched.

Shaun was quick to retaliate. 'I didn't steal shit, ya dumb slut! Even if I did, what ya gonna do about it?' Shaun jeered at his peer, ready for a fight.

Beth lunged towards Shaun and threw a punch that connected with his chin.

'Fuckin bitch!' Shaun screamed, as he flew at her and grabbed wildly at her hair.

Sarah and Jock flew straight into action, using safe restraint moves to separate the fighting residents. Jock approached Shaun from behind, holding him tight in a bear hug until he calmed down. At the same time, Sarah and Kerry approached Beth and took an arm each to lead her away from the drama. On this occasion, the incident was contained before it escalated, but there were many nights when it was not as simple. The police and paramedics often ended up on the scene, thanks to the residents inflicting nasty injuries on each other. Sometimes they'd smash up the furniture and end up being charged with property damage. These were the most draining nights of all and often the staff at Woodies would be at work well past their finishing time, writing up critical incident reports, making sure affected residents were supported and more importantly, debriefing with each other afterwards. None of them ever complained, though, and Sarah often marvelled at how she'd managed to retain such wonderful dedicated staff, given the usual turnover in this type of work. Unless one worked in that environment, it was difficult to understand how quickly these incidents could get out of hand, regardless of the skill set of the team. Once the residents finally settled in their rooms and all the relevant critical incident paperwork was completed, the team huddled in the office.

'Is everyone ok?' Sarah addressed the group. After receiving reassuring nods all around, the debriefing session was over quickly. Sarah decided it was safe to change the subject and turned to face her staff, her almond-shaped green eyes shining with excitement as she absent-mindedly fiddled with her chestnut-coloured ponytail.

'Guys, it's time to let you in on some exciting news… Nick and I are expecting our first baby! Obviously, I didn't want to mention it until we'd been for the first scan and got the all-clear. We are so excited!'

Kerry clapped a hand over her open mouth clearly not expecting this news. 'That's so amazing, Sarah! Congratulations. I didn't even know you were trying to get pregnant!' The two women hugged while grinning from ear to ear.

Jock flashed a broad smile. 'That's gid news, hen! Dae ye ken whit sex the bairn will be?' Kerry and Sarah looked at Jock blankly, their bewildered expressions making him rock backwards on his heels with mirth.

'Can't you speak basic English so that we Aussies can understand you for once, mate?' Kerry winked at Jock, who in turn put on his mock 'I'm so offended' face.

Jock rolled his eyes and pointed to Sarah's belly. 'It's a simple question: dae ye ken if it's a boy or a girl?'

Kerry looked confused. 'My great grandparents were Scottish, and they used the word wean for a child, but you are saying bairn. Are there different words meaning the same thing in Scotland, then?'

Jock chuckled. 'It aw depends on where ye live in Scotland, as tae which word ye use. The word wean comes fae the west o' Scotland and is a cross between the words wee and one.'

Kerry looked fascinated. 'Ah, that explains it, as my great grandparents were from Glasgow. I love hearing how all these weird and wonderful old-fashioned words came about!'

Jock clapped his hands, clearly enjoying educating the team about his Scottish roots. He looked at Sarah pointedly, 'So, when are ye gonna skedaddle?'

Sarah folded her arms in mock exasperation. 'Okay Jock, now you are just showing off. You know perfectly well that I would have no idea what the hell that means!'

Jock chuckled; he loved to wind his colleagues up. 'It means when are ye leaving us?' His face went serious for a minute. 'Have ye thought aboot when ye will tell the residents and aboot how we keep ye safe till ye go on maternity leave? Ye cannae be stepping in to stop fights anymore, lassie… um like you did just then!'

Sarah flapped a hand dismissively. 'Jeez, you are a worrywart, just like Nick. Don't stress; I won't put myself at risk. I was hoping to put off telling the residents until it's more obvious. I will also take maternity leave a bit earlier than usual just to be on the safe side. Happy?' Sarah cocked her head to one side with a cheeky smirk as she waited for Jock's reply.

Jock's expression remained unusually serious. He scratched his shiny bald head while contemplating his response. 'Ma concern is that ah ken whit ye are like. I dinnae think ye can help yersel but get involved when there is a crisis at the unit. I'm jist worried that ye will step in withoot thinking and maybe put yersel and the bairn at risk. Yer a wee pocket rocket, hen!'

Sarah smiled. Jock often used this term of endearment given that she was petite with a slight build, but ironically she was often the first to step in and stop any fights at the unit.

Kerry nodded her head vigorously. 'I gotta say, Sarah, I agree with Jock. Obviously, you are the boss, but even tonight could have ended badly. You know as well as I do that staff can end up being punched and kicked when intervening with our little darlings. I think you should take a back seat and try to stay in the office for the duration of your shifts. Let the rest of us handle whatever is going on.'

Sarah nodded thoughtfully and gave a small salute. 'I have very astute staff and I respectfully take on board your concerns! Do you really think I need to be hands-off as early as right now, though? You know how much I like to roll my sleeves up and muck in to help.'

'Yes!' cried Jock and Kerry in unison. Sarah was touched at their concern and given that she was getting the same message at home from Nick, she began to follow their well-meaning advice and disengage from the residents. In the process, she completely underestimated how they would perceive the change in her behaviour and hold it against her.

Over the next few weeks, the residents noticed that Sarah was less involved and had taken a step back from her usual level of engagement. The older residents were becoming increasingly resentful towards her as a result. Being super sensitive to how the world perceived them, they were well attuned to any changes in the habits of the staff. Due to their low self-esteem, they were quick to assume that the changes in Sarah's behaviour implied she no longer cared about them.

One night when they were waiting for the cook to serve dinner, Beth started with the conspiracy theories. The unit troublemaker turned to the other residents waiting in line for their food and sneered at them.

'Have you guys noticed Sarah doesn't give a shit about any of us anymore? I heard she's had enough of us and thinks we are all fuckheads!'

Shaun stiffened. 'What the fuck, Beth? What makes you say that?'

Beth yawned and inspected her long black nails. 'It's pretty fucking obvious Shaun! The bitch barely looks our way anymore! So much for telling us we can always count on her! The fucking hoe has mentally checked out on us!'

Shaun kept listening but did not comment further. His cold flat grey eyes studied Beth's small mouth as she spoke in her usual bitter tone. He noted how, as usual, the others joined in like sheep. They hung on to her every word, nodding in agreement for fear of getting on the wrong side of her. Shaun couldn't stand any of them; he felt zero interest in any of the weirdos he cohabited with. People were always surprised to find out that kids who ended up living in care together rarely became close. Being in the same boat meant they should understand and support each other, but Shaun's reality was that they were just a bunch of fucked-up losers who saw each other as either a threat or as competition. They stole from each other, attacked and abused each other and certainly didn't trust each other. They all wanted the youth workers all to themselves. Who the hell wanted to share them with the other deadbeats?

But Sarah was on a different level… she was special. Sarah never failed to treat Shaun like a real human being. Sarah was an angel who never judged his past or his current behaviour, even when it was despicable and he ended up hating himself. The happy-go-lucky Woodies manager was the one who looked for the good in him, found his strengths and encouraged him to strive for achievement-based goals to increase his self-esteem. Sarah was the only woman who'd behaved maternally towards him since his dad had murdered his mum. Well, there was one other female in that category, but she'd let him down too. *Forget about her; don't even go there.*

Shaun tried hard not to dwell on his horrific childhood and felt it was easier to push away the thoughts that plagued him. If he allowed himself to go there, the memories were capable of bringing him to his knees. This used to happen often during his younger years. At one point, Shaun thought he would die from the pain and grief. His therapist at the time had pulled him from the brink but now he wondered what it had achieved in the long run. He was still a miserable twisted motherfucker and that was not about to change.

Shaun hoped for his sake that Beth was just doing her usual shit-stirring with her comments about Sarah, although the more he thought about it, the more he realised there was a great deal of truth in the rumours the stupid mutt was spreading. Sarah was definitely being less attentive and was engaging very little with any of them – if at all – of late. Shaun felt an iciness envelope him. Well if that was the way Sarah wanted to play it, she'd regret it, big time. Maybe she wasn't who he thought she was after all. Perhaps the way his dad had viewed women was accurate. His dad often used the c-word to describe Shaun's mum and now he was starting to think his dad was right. *Women are all lying bitches!*

After dinner that night, Shaun went to his room and spoke to the imaginary mates he'd formed a rock band with. Like him, they were aliens presenting as humans. They made him feel better and let him know he was not the only one who wasn't normal. Through his song writing, he would create a new way of living and a new type of love. Not that he had a clue what love meant. He'd never experienced it. Love was just a word that he liked the sound of. He sang out the haunting lyrics to the song he'd penned only a few nights before:

No one must know why we're in this world
Mustn't know that we're not people,

No one must know why we lie there curled, motionless and quite unstable
This leads to a new love, yes, a brand new love
A love that fills the air. A love that fills the air.

Everyone will soon know of this love
It's a new love in every way
Everyone will breathe this brand new love, yeah, cause it has come to stay
This leads to a new love, yes, a brand new love
A love that fills the air. A love that fills the air.

Penning lyrics made Shaun sleepy. He lay on top of the thin duvet and placed his head on the wafer-thin pillow. Shaun saw no point in getting under the duvet as it was cheap and nasty and didn't keep him warm anyway. Within minutes, Shaun was dreaming about his childhood again. Sometimes he had nightmares about his mum being murdered by his dad and other times his subconscious tapped into the few happy times he'd experienced as a child. Tonight, he was having one of his recurring dreams about the good old times with Kate.

Both Kate and the school principal had made several reports to the Child Abuse Report Line to raise concerns of neglect and physical abuse and knew that, as a result, Shaun's family was referred to another agency who did early intervention work with at-risk families. No one was convinced that the agency was having much success in engaging with the family, but at least the concerned parties knew they were on someone's radar and hopefully being monitored somehow. As much as Kate did not want children herself, she did feel protective of the poor little mite who lived next-door.

Shaun thrashed around in his bed as his vivid dream took over his subconscious. He was six years old and sitting alone in the backyard, picking at tufts of grass on the small, barren lawn with his grubby fingers. He was cold and hungry, and his bottom was numb from sitting on the hard ground for so long. His parents were late coming home, but he was used to it now. They would appear eventually but he would never know when. Shaun knew that they played pokies and drank beer at the pub but was confused about what that meant and why he was never invited. In many ways it was better when they were not there as it meant he didn't need to listen to them screaming at each other or beating each other up. Sometimes he would get in their way and they would hit him too, so he'd got better at disappearing to his hiding spot.

'Hey there, little fella!' Kate's smiling face appeared over the low fence separating their front yards. Shaun glanced up and gave his neighbour a weak smile. The young woman noted the dark circles under his eyes and how thin he was looking. Her heart went out to the boy. 'Hey, I'm going to the McDonald's Drive Thru. Do you fancy a happy meal on me?' Shaun's gaunt face lit up and he nodded eagerly at the offer. He hadn't eaten much since breakfast time the day before and his stomach was rumbling horribly. Kate knew she risked offending the boy's parents when she helped him out, but she rarely saw them or if she did, they were often too drunk to notice that she was occasionally feeding their child.

'I'll be back in ten minutes!' Shaun gave an eager wave as Kate jumped into her car and backed out of her driveway. His neighbour hadn't really intended to go to McDonald's to buy dinner but felt compelled to feed the little boy and knew most kids loved to eat burgers and chips.

When she returned, Shaun came and sat with her on her porch where they ate together and chatted away. Kate continually glanced nervously over to her neighbour's house. She was rather intimidated by the volatile couple who lived there and worried about them abusing her for interfering in their lives. Kate was careful never to invite Shaun inside; instead, they would remain on her porch until his parents appeared. Most of the time, he would slip unnoticed back into his own yard. As his parents were loud and argumentative, their presence in the street was often noted well before they appeared at their front door.

Shaun savoured the pleasant dream. He was back sitting on Kate's porch enjoying every morsel of the burger he was munching. When they ran out of things to say, he knew it meant that Kate wanted to go back inside her house, but she didn't, because she was afraid of leaving him alone, especially when it became dark outside. Even at such a tender age, he knew intuitively that Kate cared about him and was putting his needs before her own. It stood out to him because it was so different to what he'd experienced with his own parents.

When the conversation dried up, Shaun would stare pointedly at her garden gnome with the broken arm. It became his only other friend. He didn't want to talk to it out loud, so he'd send his thoughts to it through his mind and hoped it received them somehow.

'Hi Mr Gnome. I get scared and feel sad and lonely. I want my mum and dad to stop fighting and stay at home with me. Can you help me, Mr Gnome? Can you? Please? I will try to be a good boy even though I enjoy being bad. When I go to school the other kids tease me because I look dirty and my uniform is ripped. Can you get me a new uniform, Mr Gnome? Can you, please? Can you make sure Mum takes me to school? Because she only takes me sometimes. I like to go because I can steal other kids' recess snacks when my tummy rumbles. Thanks for listening, Mr Gnome.'

Shaun smiled in his sleep; he could almost taste the burger Kate bought for him. But then his face turned into a worried frown and he yelled out, 'Nooo!' Shaun woke up with a start, his heart thudding. Even to this day, his loser parents managed to continue ruining his life. The dream usually ended when they returned home drunk and started bashing each other. Shaun's job was to keep quiet and keep out of their way. His moment of blissful slumber was broken. Why the fuck did any pleasant dreams always have to take a turn for the worse?

CHAPTER 6

A few days later, Sarah was enjoying her day off and was floating around in a happy bubble, completely oblivious to the conversations the residents were having about her at Woodies. She'd just had her hair done and it fell around her shoulders in glossy chestnut-coloured waves. Her clothes were starting to feel a little tight, so she was at Rundle Mall looking for trendy oversized attire. She hoped to find something comfortable that would conceal her pregnancy but not look like an obvious maternity outfit. Eventually she settled on a longline oversized fluffy orange cardigan. She admired herself from all angles in the changing room mirror at the Myer store. Sarah noted the style of the cut hung well and would easily conceal her expanding girth. Sarah let out a soft chuckle. She could tell she would become attached to the cardigan; she tended to do that with fluffy clothes. Sarah smiled as she thought she wouldn't be at all surprised if she was still obsessed with the cardigan in years to come. She'd never understood women who only wore clothes for one season.

As Sarah headed for the tram stop on King William Street to head home, she considered how easy it'd been so far to stay mainly in the office at work. It took a fair bit of willpower to avoid becoming involved with any outings or incidents with the residents. Navigating the workplace while pregnant was easier than she'd thought and she felt pleased with herself. Her protective instincts had automatically kicked in when her belly began to swell. The changes to her body were still not obvious to others if she dressed carefully, but she knew she'd need to sit down with the team soon to work out the date when she should go on maternity leave. Sarah's colleagues and husband were somewhat relieved that she'd finally seen sense. She smiled dreamily as she thought about how lucky she was to have so many people in her life who cared. The baby would be the first grandchild on both sides of the family and would no doubt be suitably spoiled.

There were a few things she was yet to finalise before she could even think about going on maternity leave for a year, though. As the tram pulled in and Sarah settled into a seat, she started a mental checklist in her head. *I need to prepare for Shaun's upcoming eighteenth birthday, complete his leaving care plan and make sure we are on track with securing his independent living accommodation. I may need to delegate that job to Jock… I need to make sure his last week at Woodies is special for him given that I can't be there… Corey needs to be booked into the camp he wants to attend. I need to speak to his social worker about the camping gear he needs. Beth is also close to reaching independence. I have a zillion things I need to organise for her. We have a new resident arriving soon, too. I must read his file and get an understanding of his history…*

Sarah's thoughts eventually tired her out, and she was embarrassed to wake up a few minutes later due to her head jerking her awake. She licked the drool that had formed at the corners of her mouth before giving the other passengers a furtive glance. *How embarrassing that I nodded off! Looks like no one noticed. This pregnancy lark is exhausting!*

Later that evening, after stuffing her face with Nick's famous ricotta-stuffed pasta shells drizzled with tomato sugo, Sarah flopped on the sofa in front of the television. Nick joined her and they snuggled close, both feeling contented with life. Sarah suddenly jerked upwards, an excited grin lighting up her dainty features. 'I felt a ripple in my belly!' She pulled her oversized T-shirt upwards with excitement. Nick's enthusiasm matched hers. 'Oh my god, let me see!' He placed his face right next to her belly, making her laugh heartily.

They both stared at her belly, willing the baby to move again. After a minute or so, Nick was defeated, 'Looks like bubs is playing hide and seek, cheeky thing!' Sarah was about to pull her T-shirt back down when they both saw a clear ripple across her belly. 'Did you see that!' they both cried in unison before they both burst into fits of excited squeals.

As their laughter subsided, Sarah looked at her husband, her green eyes matching his tender blue ones. 'How did we get to be so damn lucky?' Nick kissed the top of her head. 'I dunno, babe. I'm the happiest man on earth right now.'

CHAPTER 7

The weeks flew by and it became increasingly difficult for Sarah to hide her pregnancy at work. She considered being upfront and telling the residents she was expecting a baby but after hearing a horror story about what had happened to a colleague at one of the residential care units on the other side of town, she'd decided not to. A youth worker named Amanda had decided to be upfront about her pregnancy and the youths she worked with had become increasingly jealous and vindictive as her bump grew.

One of the residents, Clarice, was particularly bitter about Amanda going on maternity leave. Clarice felt hard done by that her favourite youth worker would be leaving to care for her own child instead of her. One day she'd become vicious towards Amanda, completely out of the blue. Clarice had run up to Amanda and kicked her straight in the stomach with a Doc Martens-booted foot. Amanda had been rushed to hospital due to placental abruption and required an emergency Caesarean section to save the baby.

Sarah did not want to put herself at risk of anything similar happening during the last trimester of her pregnancy. Therefore, she decided she would quietly slip out of Woodies when the time came to start her maternity leave. Sarah intended to brainstorm with the team about what to tell the residents about her sudden disappearance. She knew they would be hugely impacted by her absence, but she was more than confident that Jock would be a success as acting manager. Sarah grinned as she was about to let Jock know he'd won the position for the short-term contract to cover her maternity leave.

As if on cue, Jock strolled into the office and greeted her with a wide smile. 'Now then! Chuck the kettle on, hen. Let's sit doon and hae a wee blether!' Sarah smiled; she'd finally remembered that blether was a Scottish word meaning to chat. 'Yes, we do need to have a chat, Jock. I have some exciting news for you!' Jock sat across from her, his eyes wide with anticipation. 'Spill the beans then, hen!' Sarah chuckled; she'd still never fathomed out why calling a female a hen was a term of endearment in Scotland. She found this rather cute all the same.

Sarah put on her best official voice. 'I'd like to inform you that you are the successful candidate to act as manager for the year when I go on maternity leave. Congratulations, Jock! Or should I use your official title: Mr Martin 'Jock' Richardson?'

Jock rubbed his hands together with glee. 'Aww shucks, that's gid news, hen. Thanks very much!' Sarah laughed. 'It's well deserved, my friend. The work you do with these young people is nothing short of incredible! The feedback we get about the camps you run is phenomenal! Not to mention that you are just an all-round bloody good bloke and funny, to boot!' Jock put on a mock humble face. 'Jings! Ye will be giving me a big heid at this rate!' They both laughed; she was finally understanding most of the Scottish lingo.

Once the rest of the staff shuffled in and were seated for the monthly team meeting, Sarah announced that Jock would be acting as the Woodies manager. The response from the team was several whoops of approval, which she was pleased about. Obviously, the other candidates would be disappointed; but no one could deny Jock was more than worthy of the opportunity. He was such a great bloke; it would be difficult for anyone not to wish him every success.

Jock addressed the team. 'I'm chuffed at having the chance tae act up as manager, guys. Now a ken I'm the office clown, but in aw seriousness, if there's anything ye want to address either aboot the kids' wellbeing or yer own… well ye ken where tae find me. Ma door will always be open, okay?'

The team spent a few minutes giving approving nods and words of congratulations. Sarah let Jock have his minute of glory and receive a few playful thumps on the back from the others before moving on with the agenda.

'Okay, now for the next bit of news, folks.' Sarah's tone became more serious. I've decided, after much nagging from Nick and considering what happened to Amanda whilst pregnant, that I will leave earlier than planned. So, I'm now going to finish up on Friday this week. This decision has also been driven by my doctor, who says my blood pressure is too high. So I have to take that on board with immediate effect. Of course, that means I need Jock to step up a little earlier than planned.'

Jock raised his eyebrows in mock horror, but Sarah knew he was teasing her. There were a few audible gasps around the room. Everyone knew how much work Sarah did behind the scenes and there would be a fair bit of delegation happening to ensure all the young people received the services they required if she left so soon. Kerry was secretly resentful of the timing because both Beth and Shaun would require a lot of one on one assistance in the lead up to leaving care. Sarah was usually the one that prepared a lot of the discharge paperwork and it was unlikely she'd delegate it all to Jock. Kerry knew deep down that if she was in Sarah's shoes, she'd have done the same thing so she tried to push the unwelcome thoughts to one side. *How can I grudge my manager going on well-deserved maternity leave? Maybe I'm more stressed and overloaded than I realised!*

Despite the extra work they'd have to undertake, after a few seconds of contemplation, everyone reassured Sarah they approved of her plan and her reasons for it. Kerry continued to look pensive, however, and Sarah was quick to notice. 'Are you okay, Kerry? What are you thinking?'

Kerry nodded slowly. 'I just think we need to be really smart about this. I mean we haven't told the kids a thing about your pregnancy and they don't know your departure is imminent. We all know you will be sorely missed and that they are bound to hold it against you for not telling them you are going.'

Sarah grimaced. 'I've tossed and turned about this dilemma. There is no good way to step out of their lives, particularly as I've worked with many of them for a number of years. But what do I say? Do I pretend I have another job? They'd be devastated. Do I say that I want to leave for a bit? I just don't know how to frame that to them. They are so sensitive and most of them have suffered enough grief and loss to last a lifetime. There is no way I want them to know about the baby. Look at what Shaun did to that toddler all those years ago! Not to mention what happened to poor Amanda when she told the kids at work about her pregnancy! These young people are just too volatile and unpredictable, and I'd rather keep my private life separate from them.'

Jock nodded in agreement. 'There's nae easy solution tae this at all, but I dinnae think that just slinking oot the door is the right thing tae do either. They will feel betrayed if you just disappear off the face of the earth. Shaun is gonnae take this the hardest oot of all of them. It's a shame yer going before he exits Woodies. He is so close tae turning eighteen, it's almost a crime that the timing is so off.'

Sarah sighed. 'Okay. You are right, Jock. What was I thinking? I need to let them know I'm going, but no matter how I frame it they will see it as yet another rejection. It makes me feel awful and so damn guilty.' As a barrage of protests started up from the team about how she should never feel guilty, Sarah put her hands up in mock surrender.

'Okay, guys. Simmer down. I know I have nothing to feel bad about! It's just difficult not to feel that way. These are highly damaged young people and they are not going to like my departure one little bit.'

Kerry piped up. 'I know! Why don't we ask the cook to do pizzas this Friday night and you can announce it then? We know from past staff departures that the kids tend not to fare too well with any sort of build up to them leaving. The anticipation of how their absence will affect them only makes things worse. The crazy behaviours and critical incidents tend to escalate when a staff member leaves. I'd suggest that you tell them during dinner and let us deal with the aftermath over the weekend.'

Several murmurs of agreement with Kerry's idea could be heard around the table. Sarah's face took on a pained expression, her concern evident in her green eyes. 'I can't believe how hard it is to come up with the right thing to say to them. All ideas will be gratefully received! But realistically, no one will be able to find a way to sugar-coat it.' Jock nodded and thought to himself: *The matriarch is leaving and maybe she will never return.*

CHAPTER 8

Friday night came around quickly and Sarah found herself at the dinner table for the last time with the young people of Woodies. Her palms were sweaty as she struggled to find the right words to let them know she was leaving. She knew she was like a mother figure to the residents and her news would not go down well, regardless of how she tried to frame it.

Sarah clutched her orange cardigan protectively around her middle and watched the residents have their usual squabbles over the various types of pizza on offer. They greedily snatched up the slices from the serving platters and wolfed them down, despite knowing staff would ensure they all received equal servings. Watching them scrabbling for food still made Sarah sad. *It was a survival tactic that had become ingrained after being neglected and starved before coming into care.*

Jock could sense that Sarah needed to get her speech over and done with as soon as possible. He was in tune with her ways after working alongside her for so long. Jock knew when Sarah was out of her comfort zone and he willed her to get her speech right. Most of the kids were already licking their fingers, ready to get started on the Friday night activities. Jock decided to get the ball rolling. 'Okay guys, listen up.' The residents stopped talking and glanced up, hoping Jock had a fun activity lined up.

Satisfied that he had their full attention he looked over at Sarah who shrugged and mouthed, 'It's now or never.' Jock's face was unusually serious, and Corey's tummy suddenly felt tight. Something was up; Jock was looking pointedly at Sarah.

'I have some news.' Sarah paused, her usual confident voice sounding squeaky and uncertain. The words she'd rehearsed came out completely differently. 'I… uh, my husband has been told he has to work in Melbourne and… uh, it means I have to go with him. Um, we need to go next week and so… uh, I might be away from Woodies for a year or so.' *Why am I lying to them? Because I still have to get out of here in one piece, that's why!*

A stunned silence followed. Sarah lowered her eyes, not enjoying having several sets of critical eyes boring into her. She took a deep breath. 'I know that means I will miss various important moments for you all, but I can get the staff to FaceTime me and I….'

Beth began to clap her hands, slowly and sarcastically to drown out Sarah's voice. 'Well, whaddya fucking know!' Her eyes swept the room knowingly. 'I told you the useless two-faced mutt didn't give a shit about us anymore! Well, there you go; I was right! She is pissing off and leaving us all to rot! Well done, Sarah. Your news has gone down like a fucking lead balloon!' Beth pointed a finger accusingly at Sarah, her long black talon-like nails just as imposing as her glittering dark eyes. 'You turned out be a piece of shit just like everyone else that abandoned us! I'm on my eighth fucking social worker and now you are about to fuck off too! Well, good fucking riddance!' Sarah opened her mouth to respond but found she was lost for words as a miserable expression formed on her usual smiley face. *I can't insult Beth's intelligence by disagreeing with what she is saying because it's all true.* Sarah gulped, willing at least one of the residents to say something positive.

Corey sat there stunned, a massive lump forming in his throat, which he quickly swallowed down but not before Jock noticed the look of hurt and rejection in his eyes. Jock made a mental note to continue reading the *Harry Potter* books to him in Sarah's absence.

Poor kid; he is still so young and fragile. I hope Sarah didn't see that look on his face because it will kill her inside if she did.

As the negative reactions created a ripple effect, mayhem ensued, and the residents began yelling various abusive comments at Sarah who by this point was openly crying. No residents listened as the staff tried hard to stop the situation from escalating. Sarah looked on helplessly as her years of hard work and the respect she'd earned from the residents began to crumble all around her. *Why does this have to be so hard?*

Shaun sat in silence, his heart beating wildly but his face giving nothing away. He stared at Sarah with his flat grey eyes, willing her to be joking, to take back what she'd said. He experienced the same thought repeatedly, on a loop: *She won't be here for my eighteenth birthday or my last day at Woodies. How could she do something as devastating as this to me?*

Sarah felt Shaun's stare penetrate through her and she stood up abruptly. Enough was enough; she was beginning to feel intimidated.

'I need to use the bathroom' she muttered. Sarah bolted to the office, grabbed the last of her things and headed straight to the car park without turning back. She hated leaving this way and could not have imagined a worse exit.

Why couldn't I work in a normal job where you have a nice afternoon tea when you go on maternity leave? Because these are severely damaged young people and it was my choice to work with them, that's why. Surely on some level they care about me even though they are completely incapable of showing it? Maybe they care about me too much, more than I ever realised. Now they will hate me, and I can't do a damn thing about it!

As Sarah carefully strapped her seatbelt over her growing baby bump, she surmised that unless you'd worked in a care setting where, to the residents, you were their lifeline, you simply wouldn't understand it. She seriously considered running back into Woodies and telling them she'd made a mistake, that she'd stay on until she gave birth, and remain present for all of the residents' upcoming milestones. But the damage was done. She would be unable to turn back now.

Sarah sincerely hoped that Nick would get her through this period in her life as she was one big emotional wreck right now. She placed a protective hand on her belly. *Surely my current state of mind isn't good for the baby?* Sarah could not remember the drive home, but she was aware of the salty taste of her tears as they streamed rapidly down her face.

CHAPTER 9

Good Friday 2021

Sarah and Nick exchanged excited grins as they locked up their house and packed the family car in preparation for their Easter trip. Life had been so busy since they'd become parents. A trip away would do them good.

'I'm so keen for some quality family time,' Sarah smiled at her husband as she hopped into the passenger side of their Mazda CX9. Nick nodded in agreement.

'Yup. Long overdue, hey? But wait, are you just looking forward to family time?' He glanced at her with a twinkle in his eyes. 'What about factoring in a bit of couple time too?' He squeezed Sarah's knee suggestively as he expertly navigated their car through the narrow driveway into the street. Sarah batted her eyes and put on her best girlish giggle.

'Well, now that you mention it, I thought it might be a good time to try for baby number two. It's been a few weeks since I stopped taking the pill so I should be good to go! If my parents and sister are keen to entertain Finn for a bit, we might be in with a chance of special alone time.'

Nick gave his wife a furtive glance; she was looking good. Her toned thighs were on display, thanks to the khaki mini-dress she was sporting. He'd be up for a bit of afternoon delight, given half the chance. Life was good and he was one lucky man. *A few days away from the office and quality time with my wife, son and the in-laws. What more could a man want?*

Feeling young and free, they turned the music up and sang along to the nineties tunes playing on the radio. Despite the amount of traffic on the roads, they made good time. When they finally pulled into the driveway of the rental property they would call home for the next few days, they were both more than ready for a few days of reprieve from their hectic lives. It'd been an enjoyable drive from Adelaide down to Port Elliot. Their two-year-old son, Finn, was travelling in his auntie Jessica's car, which was a novelty for him and allowed for some much-needed peace and quiet for them. Sarah knew only too well that her sister would have spoiled Finn during the trip with various snacks and no doubt an ice cream stop on the way.

Finn adored his auntie Jessica. She was the next best thing to his mummy. Given that Sarah and Jessica were only nineteen months apart in age and physically similar, they were often mistaken for twins. The sisters were close confidants and often shared their woes with each other. Jessica loved Finn as though he were her own child.

The annual trip to Port Elliot with the wider family was predictable but always a lot of fun. Sarah and Nick arrived at the holiday home only ten minutes after Sarah's parents, who'd come running down the path to meet them with their arms outstretched.

'Aw you guys are too cute' laughed Sarah as she and Nick exchanged hugs with her mum and dad.

Nick smiled. 'Jeez, no one would believe we only actually live half an hour away from each other in Adelaide!'

Jean and Paul Henderson exchanged sheepish grins as they helped their daughter and son-in-law grab their bags and provisions from the boot of their car. Paul ran a hand through his thick white hair as he carried in his daughter's Country Road weekend bag on his other shoulder.

Paul glanced back at the younger couple. 'Well, don't be too hard on us oldies for getting excited. You guys are always so busy and we don't get to see you as much as we'd like to. So let us enjoy you while we can!' Jean nodded her head vigorously in agreement as she put an arm around Sarah's shoulder.

'Your dad's right; we do get a bit carried away at having everyone together, even if it is just for the long weekend. Nick did a good job choosing this year's holiday home. It's lovely!'

After a satisfying tour of the rental house, which met with everyone's approval, Sarah flopped onto a candy-striped deckchair on the patio.

'Well, I don't know about anyone else, but I'm going to enjoy a glass of bubbles while we still have peace and quiet before Jessica and Finn arrive!' she said.

Jean clapped her hands in delight 'Great idea, darling! I already have a bottle chilling in the fridge.'

Paul smiled affectionately at his wife. 'You sit down, and I will get you girls the champers. Do you want to grab a couple of beers for us from the Esky, Nick?'

As the two men sauntered off, Jean felt her heart swell and her eyes fill with tears. 'How did I get so lucky to have all of you in my life?'

Sarah leaned forward and squeezed her mum's hand. 'Aw Mum, you are so sentimental these days. We are so lucky to have you too. Family time is precious – you have always taught us that – and we will always keep this tradition of going away at Easter together.'

Jean looked at Sarah with glassy eyes. 'Promise?' Sarah laughed at her mum's childish expression.

'I promise, Mum!' Jean hiccupped and Sarah narrowed her eyes. 'Have you drunk some bubbles already, Mum?'

Jean shrugged and giggled, indicating that she had, but put her index finger to her lips as a sign to Sarah to keep it quiet. 'Shhh!' Jean winked at her daughter, a mischievous grin lighting up her wizened features. 'I had a drink on the way here, but your dad thought my mini-bottle of Prosecco was a soft drink when I knocked it back in the car.' Jean looked proud of her trickery and Sarah shook her head in mock horror. When Paul and Nick returned with a tray of drinks, they were baffled by the two women laughing like a pair of hyenas. The men exchanged a puzzled look and everyone clinked glasses.

A few minutes later Finn burst through the door clutching his new PAW Patrol Dino Rescue Patroller toy. Jessica trailed behind him, lugging a Country Road weekender bag identical to her sister's, a huge grin on her face as she watched Finn demonstrate with great gusto what his new present from his auntie could do. Paul and Nick were quick to channel their inner child and join Finn on the floor to play with the motorised vehicle that moved at the touch of a button.

Sarah handed her sister a glass of bubbles. 'Thanks so much for letting Finn come in your car, and for spoiling him. You really are the best auntie!' She smiled appreciatively at her son, husband and dad who were now huddled together on the rug in the lounge room. Jessica's eyes shone. 'I loved every minute, sis; my nephew is such a cutie pie! I also thought rather than giving him a ton of chocolate at Easter, I'd get him a practical gift instead.'

Sarah smirked. 'So, you didn't bring any chocolate eggs for him?'

Both women laughed in unison as they knew perfectly well that the weekend would end up being a chocolate fest, not just for Finn but for all of them, given that their ingrained family Easter egg hunt tradition was hard to break. Sarah didn't like her son to overindulge, but she made exceptions at family gatherings because she knew she would be fighting a losing battle if she tried to challenge her family members.

Finn was advanced for a two-year-old, which Sarah attributed to her extensive knowledge of child development. His fine and gross motor skills were well developed, and his speech was coming on a treat. She watched her son play with his relatives and her heart swelled with pride. She was excited to try for another baby, yet she honestly questioned whether she could love another child as much as Finn. Her friends assured her that this was a normal feeling, however, and that she'd find all the love she needed within her as soon as the new baby appeared.

Nick came up behind his wife and massaged her shoulders. Sarah glanced upwards over her shoulder at her handsome husband and their eyes locked. He whispered softly into her ear. 'Are you thinking what I'm thinking?' He gave his best sexy grin. Sarah nodded, suddenly feeling overcome with desire. They made their excuses to the family about needing a mini-nap after the drive and slunk off to the guest bedroom they'd been assigned. They knew Finn was too engrossed in showing off his new toy to his grandparents to notice if they disappeared for a bit.

As Nick locked the door behind him, Sarah slipped her dress up over her head revealing that she was naked underneath. Nick gasped as he drank her in for a few seconds: her pert breasts, tiny waist and the curve of her hips. He began stripping off as he moved closer to her. They kissed slowly as he held her face with both hands, his broad shoulders and muscular arms turning her to jelly. Nick wanted to savour every moment. He nuzzled her neck then began moving downwards, covering her in light kisses until she tingled all over.

As they fell onto the bed, they were both panting with desire and unable to draw it out any longer. As Nick entered Sarah she gasped with pleasure and her eyes suddenly filled with tears as she thought about how lucky she was. It occurred to her that she was becoming just as soppy as her mum. It made her smile; it wasn't a bad trait to value her family. She had a great marriage, a beautiful son and hopefully they would soon be blessed with another baby. Sarah believed strongly in the power of gratitude, especially after working with some of the most traumatised kids in the state.

Following their lovemaking, Nick rolled onto his side and propped himself up on his elbow, his hand cradling his handsome face. His deep blue eyes crinkled at the corners as he grinned at his wife. 'What are you so deep in thought about?' Sarah smiled back at him and flicked back the sheet as she stood up.

Sarah stretched. 'I'm thinking I could lie here with you all day, but we better get back down there to join the family before we get busted!' Nick sighed as he jumped out of the other side of the bed towards the ensuite. 'Yeah, fair enough. Let's have a quick shower and get back down there before Finn sends out a search party.'

Sarah looked at him coyly. 'We would save time if we showered together.' Nick knew where she was going with the idea and looked downwards to discover he was up for it. When Nick and Sarah eventually sauntered back downstairs with wet hair and flushed faces, it was obvious to the rest of the family that they had not in fact been napping after all.

'Mummy! Daddy!' shrieked Finn as he ran towards them.

Jean nudged her daughter in the ribs and smirked. 'He was just starting to ask where you were.'

The two women began to laugh knowingly again and once more the men looked on in bewilderment. Paul stared lovingly over at his wife and daughters as he watched their faces crease with mirth. He thought women were strange creatures, but he loved these special ones dearly. He'd never understand their secret women's business, but he was a contented man all the same.

After eating copious amounts of fresh South Australian produce including a platter of local oysters, cheeses, olives, pâtés, dips and artisan crackers, the family settled down to play a few games of charades. It was a long-standing family joke that Jessica always seemed to tag onto the losing team despite being an extra player.

Finn was tucked up in his grandparents' bed for the night and the adults were getting rowdy. Much hilarity ensued as the more wine they consumed, the less chance each team had of guessing either the proposed book or film the current player was trying to convey. Slowly but surely, everyone started to turn in for the night. Jessica was the only family member who smoked so she liked to wait up to avoid critical eyes judging her dirty habit. Sarah usually stayed up with her after everyone else had gone to bed for the night; it was good to enjoy a one-on-one chat with her sister.

'Aren't you cold?' Sarah asked Jessica as she watched her sister light up a cigarette on the patio, wearing just jeans and a singlet.

'Yeah, I am a bit,' Jessica nodded, while rubbing the goose bumps that appeared on her arms.

'Here, put my cardigan on to take the chill off.' Sarah handed Jessica her oversized orange cardigan as she'd already changed into her flannelette pyjamas and was feeling cosy.

Jessica laughed. 'I didn't think you'd part with it; you have been pretty attached to this garment for quite some time now!'

Sarah grinned. 'Yeah, I get attached to woolly things – as you know! I've been wearing this since I was pregnant with Finn! I think, after years of working in a residential care unit, I just seek comfort and that extends to my clothes too. Sounds weird, right?'

Jessica shrugged. 'Each to their own, sis. I know we're alike in many ways but the work you've done with disadvantaged young people is something I could never do. It shows you have a big heart given you managed to work with those kids for so long. It's quite an accomplishment to maintain staying power in that type of environment.' Jessica inhaled deeply on her cigarette as she pondered further. Sarah watched her sister as she blew a straight line of blue smoke upwards into the night sky.

'Don't you ever wonder if it will bite you on the ass though, Sarah? Like could these kids come forward as adults one day and try to sue the state for how messed up their lives have been, or something?'

Sarah looked perplexed. 'No, I don't worry about things that might never happen; what's the bloody point in that? It annoys me that so many people blame the state government for the way these kids turn out. They were messed up long before they came into care! The damage has already been done! The youth workers just do the best they can to build their self-esteem and help them reach their potential. Granted, we don't have nearly enough success stories, but it doesn't make it our fault either. I know I did my best with those kids while they were in care and that's all I need to know. My conscience is clear.'

'Fair enough,' Jessica yawned, suddenly feeling exhausted after all the family shenanigans.

Sarah took the hint. 'Okay, time for bed. I hope Nick isn't waiting up!' Sarah pointed to her sleep attire, alluding to her pyjamas being a mood crusher. She deliberately played down how passionate her marriage was because she was mindful that she had something her sister was still yearning for and didn't want to rub her nose in it.

The siblings giggled as they linked arms and crept quietly up the carpeted staircase. Jessica smiled dreamily. *I hope this is the year I meet 'the one'*. She was a tad envious that Sarah and Nick were so happy together. Her ultimate dream was to meet a guy as handsome and good-natured as her brother-in-law.

As if reading her thoughts, Sarah turned to face her sister. 'Before you ask; no, Nick does not have any single mates. Believe me, you would be the first to know!' Jessica rolled her eyes, realising she'd been about to ask the same predictable question she always did. Laughing softly, so as not to disturb anyone, the sisters exchanged hugs before parting ways to their respective guest bedrooms.

CHAPTER 10

Butch turned his face upwards towards the setting sun and inhaled sharply through his nostrils. The orange and red hues excited him as they symbolised the fire igniting inside of him. He considered that it was no coincidence that his intended victim was wearing her orange oversized cardigan today. He'd seen her in the passenger seat, her husband at the wheel, as they chatted like a pair of carefree love birds. Maybe she subconsciously knew the colour she should die in. After all, it was the same colour as the setting sun. The traitor was unaware that she was about to enjoy her very last sunset on earth. *What a blast!* He lowered his head and licked his lips, his breath coming in short gasps, as adrenaline flooded his six-foot lanky frame. He was surprisingly strong for someone so tall and slim.

He gave a self-satisfied nod as he stared knowingly across the horizon. By the time the sky had become a blanket of black velvet scattered with smatterings of silver, he would have achieved the first step of his plan. Butch spent many nights sleeping rough under the stars. The night sky had become strangely familiar and comforting. He looked over at the holiday home he was watching from a safe distance. Butch reached into his holdall and brought out a small glass pipe in preparation for a quick crystal meth hit. He let out a low howl of anticipation, displaying his trademark gummy smile full of corroded teeth. He reached into his bag and pulled out a black balaclava. Then he slid his hand back inside the bag and absent-mindedly fingered the sledgehammer and .38 calibre revolver to make sure they were still there. *It is almost time.*

As Butch stealthily made his way over to the holiday rental home, he realised his bag was heavier than he had first thought. He considered that if he needed to run at some point, it could potentially slow him down. He slid around to the back of the house, unlatching the side gate as quietly as he could. The house was still, and he was fairly certain everyone was asleep. He'd waited patiently for all the lights to be out and then waited a bit more. Butch raised the sledgehammer in anticipation of breaking the lock on the back door when he realised that the dumb fuckers had not even locked it. Although it made things easier, it irritated him somewhat. Were these people stupid? It also meant he would not get to practice his breaking-and-entering skills. He didn't want tonight's task to be a piece of piss. If the task was too easy then he wouldn't feel like he'd achieved anything on his own. He stealthily entered the house gripping the revolver tightly, his forearm muscles taut from the weight of the gun.

Jessica tended to experience difficulty sleeping in strange houses, even when she was as tired as she was now. She had always found it odd that during the day, a house could appear so warm and inviting, yet at night, it became instantly eerie. Ever since she was a child she'd struggled to adjust to any unfamiliar creaks and noises, when staying away from home. Jessica felt a sudden strong sixth sense that she should not undress and go to sleep in the guest bedroom tonight. She hung up Sarah's cardigan on the hook on the back of the door and looked down at her pyjamas poking out from under the pillow on the plush queen-sized bed. She smiled fondly. They were a gift from her mum, who still insisted on spoiling her girls well into their adult years. Her smile suddenly faded. *Why do I feel so conflicted about putting these PJs on?* Jessica considered that maybe her fears were due to the fact that she was the only one who slept alone on family trips, whereas Sarah had Nick to hold her in the night, while sleeping in unfamiliar surroundings. Her parents had each other too. She tutted and shook her head. *I mustn't let self-pity sneak in.*

Jessica sighed. When was her knight in shining armour going to show up? Her track record with dating decent men wasn't great. Jessica bit down on her bottom lip; it was a nervous habit she wasn't aware of. Hoping her feelings of unease would subside, she decided to sit near the window in the small armchair to try and find a bit of comfort from the moonlight before she hit the sack.

Looking out at the moonlit sky didn't help one bit; something was off with the vibe in this house. Jessica was highly attuned to a change in the energy around her. She shifted in the chair, feeling agitated. Her left eye began to twitch involuntary, a sure sign that she was stressed. But why? *Shit, I don't think I locked the back door after I finished my cigarette. My gut is telling me something bad is about to happen. I need to go back down and check that all the doors are locked!*

By the time her brain registered that she'd heard a gunshot followed by a blood-curdling scream, she desperately wanted to believe someone had got up to watch a scary television show or that it had come from somewhere afar. Jessica's heart began to thump wildly in her chest cavity, her body rigid with tension, as she tried to make a snap decision in her state of wild panic. She became aware of a soft thumping sound as though someone or something had just landed on a carpet. Jessica silently rose from the chair; she knew her hunch was right. Something was terribly wrong and she sensed there most definitely was an unwelcome guest in the house.

Butch was standing on the upstairs landing, motionless, his head cocked to one side, his eyes darting from side to side. Even though he was high, he reminded himself it was not necessary to kill everyone – only those who got in the way – and the heartbreaker herself, of course. After all, he needed the others to relive the night's horror to the cops or there would be no fun in the aftermath, would there? His head felt fuzzy; he wanted to kick himself for taking a combination of drugs that slowed his thinking down. Butch knew it was stupid to mix up his gear when tonight's mission required him to be super alert. He blinked rapidly and tried to focus on finding his intended victim. *I wish I was a terminator, a cyborg assassin sent on a mission to kill. The computer would tell me exactly where the intended target was and when to terminate. What a blast that would be!*

Jessica became aware of heavy footsteps approaching the guest bedroom she was in and she reacted with lightning speed. She bolted towards the bed, which thankfully had a large enough gap underneath it for her to slither under. The bedroom doorknob rattled, and the hinges creaked as it slowly opened. A cockroach ran over Jessica's arm and she stifled a scream with all of her might. A pair of black boots with sticky blood on them appeared in her line of sight as the intruder approached the bed. Jessica could not see the blood very well in the dark but felt sure she could smell it. It distinctly reminded her of copper.

The intruder hovered as Jessica held her breath, her lungs fit to burst. He stood still for less than a minute, but it felt like hours. She sensed him slowly looking around the room. *What is he scanning for? What or who has he come for, and why? None of us can die; please god, no!* Hot tears began to spill from Jessica's eyes as her lungs burned from holding her breath and her body trembled uncontrollably. The intruder stood there silently, remaining in the same spot for what seemed like forever. Jessica squeezed her eyes shut tight as though bracing herself for the inevitable. He was surely going to reach down and look under the bed at any moment. It would be the first place to look, would it not? Her breathing was becoming increasingly short and ragged; he was bound to hear her and then it would be game over.

A few seconds later, her eyes pinged open as she realised he was leaving the bedroom! The thud of his footsteps was heading away from her. He was definitely back out on the landing now. *I need to act quickly. I need to get to the rest of the family somehow. I must warn them, if they are still alive….*

Panic rose even higher in Jessica's throat, suffocating her and temporarily diminishing her ability to think straight. Now was not the time to hyperventilate; she needed her wits about her. *I must not allow myself to think the worst even though I know instinctively that the scream I heard only minutes before came from my mum.*

As adrenaline coursed through her veins and her flight-or-fight response kicked in, she knew she needed to act quickly and call the police. Then she could attempt to escape out of the bedroom window. The ledge would hopefully break her fall; she'd noted how wide it was earlier when they'd walked around to admire the property. Her thoughts raced erratically around in her head as a prickly fear continued to flood her body. She was determined to survive, to save her loved ones.

Jessica snatched her mobile phone from the back pocket of her jeans and hastily called triple zero. As she connected with the communications operator, Butch burst back through the door before she had a chance to speak. He'd suddenly registered the orange cardigan hanging on the back of the bedroom door on his way out. In his drug-induced state, he'd recalled that it belonged to the heartbreaker, having seen her wearing it only hours earlier while in the passenger seat of her car. As an outsider looking in, he'd sensed the intimacy between her and her husband. The smug prick was at the wheel of his fancy car, flirting with his bitch of a wife. *But not for much longer!* Butch shook his head rapidly as if to rid himself of the images that were likely to set him off in a fit of jealousy. He needed to focus on the job at hand.

At first glance he'd thought the bedroom he'd previously entered was empty and had been eager to move on to check out the adjacent room. He'd briefly considered looking under the bed but mistakenly estimated that no one could possibly fit under what appeared to be too narrow a gap. Now he quickly headed back to double check and figure out where the heartbreaker was hiding. *The heartbreaker and her prick of a husband must have heard me approaching and be somewhere nearby, cowering.*

As Butch stormed back into the dark bedroom, he charged at Jessica with full force and threw her to the floor as if she were weightless. Her mobile phone flew out of her hand across the room and Butch roared with fury upon noting that she'd managed to connect with the emergency services. An assertive female voice was on the other end. 'Emergency. Which service? Please advise whether you require police, fire or ambulance? Hello, can you hear me?' Butch promptly crushed the phone under his boot while Jessica writhed on the floor, clearly winded and gasping for breath. He no longer had the luxury of time to brutally murder his victim in the painstaking way he'd planned. He needed to escape before the police and paramedics arrived. He randomly remembered a line his high school home group teacher had used when lecturing the class about meeting their assessment deadlines. *Failing to plan, is planning to fail. Well, that's just me all over. Couldn't organise a piss up in a brewery.* As his thoughts fuelled his rage, he pummelled his fists into Jessica's face before viciously kicking her cowering body all over with his heavy boots. It was a good job he'd managed to get his hands on a gun to finish the job, now that he was time-poor. He'd stolen the gun from a well-known crook who hadn't been smart enough to hide it where it couldn't be found.

As Jessica put her hands out to defend herself, she knew she didn't stand a chance. She hadn't even found the energy to scream; her voice felt frozen in her throat. She felt the agony of each blow and willed her ordeal to be over quickly. Just seconds before Butch shot her in the chest and her life ebbed away in a pool of dark blood, the penny dropped. *I've just realised it was the orange cardigan; he must've spotted it hanging on the back of the bedroom door. The psycho saw my sister wearing it earlier and got us mixed up. He thinks I am Sarah…*

Butch looked at his handiwork and felt euphoric. The heartbreaker was dead and so was her dad. Too bad. So sad; he might still be alive if he hadn't got in his way and poked his nose in. The dude was trying to be a hero and protect his family. *How did that work out for you, old man?*

Maybe if the heartbreaker hadn't been so full of shit and hadn't pretended to care about him when she clearly didn't, then none of this would have been necessary. Feeling disgusted, he turned on his heel to leave. Butch was aware that one more bedroom remained that he hadn't entered and now he didn't have time to enjoy scaring the shit out of the occupants. He noted from a gap under the bedroom door that whoever was in there had turned the lights on. He thought he could hear frantic whispering. No doubt another triple zero call was taking place. He'd seen enough cop shows to know they would have put a trace on the first call made by the heartbreaker. Time was not on his side.

As he slunk away from the property, he felt glad his getaway vehicle was close by, but well enough hidden from sight. His bag felt even heavier than it had going in and his back was killing him. *It's time to make tracks and lay low for a bit. See if the motherfuckers can work out who did it. I kinda hope so; I deserve the recognition.*

CHAPTER 11

Senior Constable Ben Norris and Constable Leanne Evans were contemplating a stop at the local service station to buy coffee in a bid to get them through the late shift. So far it had been a reasonably uneventful night, but the downside of that was trying to stay awake when nothing was happening to get their adrenaline pumping.

'Don't keep looking at the time, Leanne. It will only make you feel worse!' scolded the more senior of the two officers.

Leanne sighed; she realised Ben made a valid point. They worked well together, but sadly, their great teamwork would soon be coming to an end. Ben had been delighted to find out a few days ago that he'd been accepted to transfer to Holden Hill police station's Criminal Investigation Branch (CIB). While he was currently on general patrols, he did have previous CIB experience. Ben realised that this type of work was where his true passions and skill set lay, hence he was eager to return. He and Leanne enjoyed working together more than either of them cared to admit but they were both too professional to make it too obvious. Just as they turned the corner and the service station came into view, the police radio crackled into life.

'Adelaide Comcen to any Victor Harbor patrol.' The two officers glanced at each other half in dismay and half in anticipation as they recognised the voice of Cheryl Peters from the police communications centre. Cheryl continued: 'Report of multiple gun shots at England Avenue, Port Elliot. It's unknown if the offender is still on the scene.'

Ben spoke rapidly into his radio. 'Victor 41; en route, lights and sirens.' Ben reached down to activate the lights and sirens as he accelerated off. *So typical! Could we not have enjoyed some refreshments first, for Christ sake! Nothing like going to a job when you are running on empty!*

During the short drive there, Ben and Leanne received confirmation of the number of the house where the alleged shootings had occurred. Cheryl advised that another call had been received, and that a scuffle had been heard before the phone went dead. A third call was then received by a woman who identified herself as Sarah Whitaker. Apparently, the woman was hysterical, but had managed to tell Cheryl her father and sister had been shot by an intruder. Ben and Leanne exchanged a grim look. Tonight was obviously going to be the shift from hell and they certainly would not be knocking off at the usual time. The police were still unclear who the shooter was or their current whereabouts. Everyone remained on edge as a result.

Ben initially parked a block away from the property so he and Leanne could assist each other to put their police vests on before they arrived on scene. As soon as Ben cut the engine and pulled up the handbrake outside the given address, he spoke into the radio.

'Victor 41. We are outside the provided address. Do we have backup on the way?'

The radio burst into life as Cheryl's voice came through loud and clear. 'The crew in Victor 42 are shutting down a rowdy party. They are still around fifteen minutes away.'

Ben and Leanne looked at each other, neither really feeling that brave about approaching the house; both secretly hoping that they'd be laughing at their unfounded fears when they knocked off later. They crept silently towards the property, Ben on the left and Leanne on the right. Leanne felt a prickle of fear. *We don't get paid enough for this shit. What are we gonna find inside this house? This doesn't feel good.*

Ben crept down the side towards the back of the house. Leanne disliked it when they needed to split up, but she needed to find the courage to stand to attention where she was. She'd only been out of the police academy for a year and was still gaining experience. A few seconds later, Ben reappeared and signalled for Leanne to follow him to the back of the house. The back door was ajar with no sign of a break in. They crept forward, crouching and shuffling on opposite sides. They entered the house and slowly proceeded to go through each room, their weapons poised at the ready. Nothing untoward was found downstairs. The scene looked innocent enough, with the remnants of a good night in the kitchen. Empty wine bottles and bowls with crumbs in them stood by the kitchen sink.

Leanne tried to steady her breathing. *Nothing of concern here so far.* With Ben in front, they crept slowly up the stairs. The grim findings on the upper landing were worse than anticipated. Leanne held in a gasp as they confirmed the lack of pulse in the two crumpled, bloody bodies located in separate bedrooms. Given that they'd searched every corner of the house and were satisfied the perpetrator was not on-site, they called in for further assistance.

Ben's hands shook slightly as he talked into his radio.

'Victor 41. The house is secure; the offender no longer appears to be on-site. We have two deceased persons, one male and one female. We also have two adult females, an adult male and a child huddled together in an upstairs bedroom. All alive and appear uninjured but in severe shock. Ambulance and backup still required, over.'

Ben and Leanne tried to shut out the images of the deceased bodies of Paul and Jessica Henderson. They had to keep it together for the sake of the rest of the family. Leanne was particularly affected by the look in Jean Henderson's eyes, which were still wild with terror. From what the officers could gather from her incoherent ramblings, the poor woman had witnessed her husband being shot and killed but the perpetrator had spared her for some reason. So far they'd ascertained that Paul had thought he'd heard a noise and when he'd climbed out of bed and opened the bedroom door, he'd been confronted by a man wearing a black balaclava. A short scuffle had taken place before Paul was shot at close range in the chest. Jean remembered screaming but the rest was a blank. This was about as much as the police could ascertain from the poor woman so far.

Jean continually rocked back and forth, her arms wrapped around her knees as she muttered incoherently. Nick and Sarah's expressions remained blank, as though they'd mentally checked out. They were simply unable to process what had taken place in such a short space of time. Their young son was glued to Sarah, with his little arms and legs wrapped around her middle as though he were hanging on for dear life. Sarah and Nick were trying to wrap their heads around why their lives had been spared, but not Paul and Jessica's. Was it a random attack or was there a motive? None of it made any sense. Leanne noted that the young couple kept going through the motions of trying to comfort the older woman but sadly it was to no avail. Leanne assessed that the remaining family members were definitely in no fit state to make sense of what had occurred there tonight.

During the searches, Leanne came across packets of hot cross buns in the pantry and she felt her eyes becoming damp. The innocence of the baked goods seemed to make the situation even more harrowing somehow. She could still envisage the pleasant evening that had taken place prior to becoming a horror show only a few hours later. Leanne could vividly imagine the anticipation the family had built up, expecting to enjoy the Easter treats they'd brought to share together the next day. Her heart became heavier still as she came across a Coles bag full of chocolate Easter eggs. *Sadly, I can't imagine anyone enjoying these now.*

Leanne couldn't help but feel a little callous as despite the severe shock the remaining family members were experiencing, they would need to give full statements as soon as possible so that police could attempt to catch the perpetrator in a timely manner. Leanne swallowed back the feeling of nausea that began to rise in her throat as she pushed away the images she'd been confronted with. For the first time, she was questioning whether she wanted to stay in the police force, long term. *If I can get through tonight, I can get through anything.*

Ben's exposure to blood and gore was commonplace to him as a police officer, but this scene had affected him more than any others he'd attended. Death became so much more personal when you could see the horror on the faces of the loved ones of the deceased. In general, Ben found it was harder to remain detached when police witnessed the direct impact on the victims. The dead woman had been beaten before being shot and it made him feel both sick and angry. *I hope that bastard's not still prowling around, watching the house. I bet he took off when he realised a triple zero call had been made, though.*

Noting that the backup crew and paramedics were on-site, Ben sighed with relief as he made his way towards them to ensure they were up to date on all of the information gathered so far. The backup crew intended to make a start on interviewing the neighbours who'd reported the shots and hopefully someone had sighted the perpetrator either arriving or leaving the property. Ben glanced at Leanne. She was doing a great job of remaining professional, but he could tell by her pale complexion and startled eyes that their grisly findings were affecting her much more than she'd care to admit. He hoped she would consider talking about the experience with a psychologist from the Employee Assistance Program even though he knew that he would not do so himself. Male officers still tended to act macho when it came to brushing off the impact of the harrowing scenes they attended. As Ben watched the paramedics wrap the four remaining victims in warm blankets in the back of the ambulance, he realised that, to date, it was the most disturbing sight either of the young police officers had experienced and the images of the murder victims would stay with them forever.

CHAPTER 12

Detective Sergeant Dylan Mathews sauntered over to the fridge and cracked open a beer. After gulping half the bottle down greedily in one hit, he came up for air and belched loudly, causing his wife Marie to give him a disapproving glance. 'Pig!' she muttered under her breath as she went back to reading a book on the sofa. Dylan ignored her; she'd been calling him a pig for years, yet she still stuck around. He couldn't be that bad after all. Dylan was making the most of his down time on his rostered days off. He gave an inward sigh. *Only another ten years until I can retire from the police force.* Dylan had been a CIB detective for way too long and was getting tired of dealing with the same bullshit investigations all the time, but it was in his blood, ingrained in his psyche. He didn't know what else to be or *how* else to be. As much as he was worn out, at the same time he thrived on it. Like many others in the force, his job became his identity. So, he wanted a reprieve but still wanted all the accolades. What was a man to do?

Dylan liked to ensure he had space to gather his thoughts, so he wandered out into the backyard to sit in the hot tub. Having an outdoor spa was one of his few indulgences and he enjoyed unwinding and thinking about unsolved cases while the jets massaged his aching body. He grunted as he lowered his stiff limbs into the inviting warm bubbles; his body creaked even during small movements these days. He'd hate to think how he'd cope doing one of the killer workouts he was renowned for back in the day. He prodded at his flabby belly and sighed. Twenty years ago, he'd boasted rock-hard abdominal muscles. Marie was a perfect size ten back then too. Neither of them had looked after themselves and it was starting to show. Dylan knew he was at the age where he should be having an overall health check, but he preferred not to face it. He had an inkling that his cholesterol was too high, and god knows what else they'd find. *Nah; ignorance is bliss.*

As his thoughts returned to the latest unsolved cases at work, he pondered on the woman from Enfield who'd come into the station recently with a pile of anonymous handwritten threatening poems she'd received in her mailbox. She was desperate to find out who was writing them and have the person charged because it was making her somewhat afraid to go about her daily life. She'd find them waiting for her when she got home from work. They were obviously hand-delivered as there were never any postage stamps on them and that was freaking her out the most. She feared the weirdo was lurking somewhere nearby and felt vulnerable knowing that he was aware of where she lived. Dylan was pleased to note that the young probationary police officer who'd taken her statement was thorough, had taken as many details as possible and had asked all the right questions. Dylan thought it was a good start, given that many of the new recruits coming out of the police academy were absolute duds these days.

Dylan was aware that the woman had taken part in quite a few online dating ventures over the last twelve months and had brushed off a few unwanted suitors, so that was where the investigation would start. Given that she'd now received eight poems in total and they were being delivered with increasing frequency, the matter needed to be taken seriously. Dylan read the poems over and over to try and ascertain clues from the content. He studied the angry-looking words written in slanted capital letters with a black biro pen. The first poem the victim had received read:

Riddle me this:
Life had meaning until one day
You upped and left and just walked away
I adored you and thought you felt the same
But to you it was all just a game

Riddle me this:
You ripped apart my heart and soul
Left a big black gaping hole
This is why you need to die
But I'm warning you – why?

Riddle me this:
I will be at your funeral and no one will know
Being there is right, they will all think so
I write when I'm high on meth
To warn of your upcoming death

The rest of the poems were increasingly sinister and all alluded to the woman's murder being imminent. The woman was advised to go and stay with friends or relatives for the time being to avoid being alone. Dylan hated giving that advice to women; it sounded condescending and was not the solution to the problem. What with all the women's rights movements and protests these days, telling women to avoid being alone or to uproot themselves in order to stay safe wasn't exactly popular advice. Dylan understood their frustration completely, but what they did not realise was that he also gave the exact same advice to men whose lives were being threatened. Whenever he tried to explain this to his wife, she would get mad and screech at him that he just didn't get what it was like to be a woman. *Nope, I won't argue with that.*

All the same, he knew his advice to this particular young woman was a token gesture and the rest of the police force knew it too, but in the meantime it was the best solution they could come up with until they caught the nasty prick posting the letters. The reality was that they simply did not have the resources to protect every potential victim in these types of scenarios, which had exploded since internet dating applications had become more popular over the last decade. However, setting up surveillance was the next step and was top of his to-do list currently.

Dylan had read the poems so many times, he almost knew them by heart. The investigating team came up with the nickname 'The Riddler' for the mystery poet, given that he started each verse with 'Riddle me this'. While the victim was sure the author of the poems was likely to be one of the men she'd dated over the last year, Dylan was less convinced. The line about attending her funeral and the Riddler's presence not being questioned by others really bothered him. It implied this person knew her on a more personal level. The woman was dismissive however and felt that this theory held no weight. Surely it was just a line put in there for shock value? No amount of open-ended questions brought forth any vital clues or concerns about the woman's immediate social network which included conversations with her friends, ex-partners, family and colleagues.

Dylan closed his eyes and rested his head against the welcome jets of water designed to massage the neck area. Given he was on rostered days off, he was well aware he should not be thinking about work. But as usual, it was pointless trying to turn his attention elsewhere because he'd never managed to achieve this in all his years on the force. Dylan knew which police officers were currently following up the leads and hoped they'd tracked down the men the victim had recently dated. This was generally the best place to start. Talking to these men might lead to a dead end but they needed to be thorough and tick all the boxes. The other thing that occurred to Dylan was that the woman might be making the whole thing up and writing the poems herself.

God knows he'd dealt with enough lunatics who would do such a thing. Only last month, he'd charged a young woman with making a false report after she was caught red-handed texting threatening messages to herself from another mobile phone. It was unbelievable the lengths that certain people would go to, just to get attention. He could not fathom how people ended up with such low self-esteem and consequent mental health issues. Still, psychology was not his gig; he would leave that stuff to the head doctors. Personally, he felt that psychologists had a way harder job than he did when it came to working people out.

After reflecting in the spa long enough for his skin to resemble a wrinkled prune, Dylan's hunch was that this particular woman was telling the truth about the delivery of the poems. The detective believed it was not easy to put on that wide-eyed breathless fear when relaying a story like that, but then again stranger things had happened. The woman would have to be one hell of an actress, though. Nine times out of ten his hunches were accurate, but he'd learned the hard way that he wasn't perfect and did get it wrong occasionally. His team knew it was important to be thorough and look at every possibility. If Dylan was honest, this complaint was a reprieve from the more heinous crimes he'd investigated lately. While the job of finding a stalker wasn't ideal, it was better than turning up to a job to find a decapitated body or one that was black from being burned to a crisp by a home-made bomb. Not much fazed Dylan; at this stage in his career, he'd pretty much seen it all. He'd face this next challenge with as much professionalism and gusto as he always did. But for now, he needed another beer.

'Marie!' he called out. He hoped his wife could hear him over the gurgle of the spa bubbles. She'd joined him out the back to enjoy the balmy night. She was sitting on a deckchair with her head buried in the racy novel she was glued to. Marie could hear him alright. But she'd got to the chapter in her book where the sexy male character was about to mount the woman and she'd be damned if her slob of a husband was going to ruin it by making her lose her train of thought. She needed to get her kicks vicariously through books because she sure as hell wasn't getting them at home anymore. Marie chose not to reply; instead she gave him a furtive glance out of the corner of her eye. She smirked when a minute later she saw Dylan easing himself out of the spa using the handrail while muttering obscenities under his breath. *Bloody hell, he looks so unfit. Are those man boobs?*

Dylan shuffled past Marie with a towel around his waist, droplets of water dripping onto the pavers along the way.

'I will get my own beer, will I?' he muttered as he reached for the handle on the sliding door leading into the main living and kitchen area.

'Make sure your feet are dry before you go in there!' his wife shrieked after him.

Dylan ignored his wife, which was not uncommon. Dylan and Marie often pretended not to hear each other. At times it turned into a contest to see who could resist answering back the most. One of the positives was that this saved any arguments from brewing because receiving no response meant the other had to disengage. They were simply playing each other at the same game.

CHAPTER 13

Butch lay in the dark, chain smoking. He really wanted to move on from the depressing unit block he was dossing in. It was full of junkie misfits and other ex-Woodies residents. The cohort was a stark reminder that this was the lifestyle he belonged to. But it was unlikely that the South Australian Housing Authority could find him anywhere better to live than this. He appeared to fit in well with the locals, but he wanted to be better than them – to be one up on them, so to speak. His ultimate goal had been to kill someone. He'd finally accomplished this. But if he was on anyone's radar then he was yet to find out about it. He had mixed feelings about that. Given that he'd stolen the gun he'd used, it was probably just a matter of time before the local bikies started sniffing around for it. He wondered if he would be caught on both counts.

Butch's initial euphoria was short-lived. He'd felt powerful committing the murders at the time but the high hadn't lasted as long as he had anticipated, nor did he feel the sense of satisfaction he had expected. He was mighty pissed off about that. He thought back to that fateful night at Port Elliot. Following the completion of his mission, he'd driven like a bat out of hell back to Ferryden Park to return the crappy Toyota Corolla he'd borrowed from a local prostitute named Loretta.

Butch intended to leave the car keys in Loretta's mailbox and get the hell out of there, given that he had blood on his clothes and boots. But in his heightened and drug-affected state, he'd decided he could do with one more favour from Loretta. He'd let himself into her unit, shaking his head at her lack of security. *The dumb bitch should be locking her door. I've just committed murder, for fuck's sake!*

Loretta's bedroom door was ajar as Butch entered and he could see the bare ass of her latest client pumping away at her. As the man climaxed and rolled over, he leapt up in fright when he saw Butch standing in the doorway staring at him menacingly. Loretta was completely stoned and appeared unperturbed.

'You bring my car back in one piece, Butch?' Loretta seemed to live in a permanently disassociated state. Drool dribbled down one side of her mouth as she slurred, her words long and drawn out.

Butch nodded, his eyes never leaving her latest client who was jumping into his clothes as fast as he could. He assumed Butch was Loretta's pimp and was keen to get his wallet out to prove he was ready to pay. The man opened his mouth to speak, then thought better of it. By not engaging with the intimidating brute, he might get out of there quicker and avoid any conflict. The man made a point of counting out the going rate and laid it on the bedside table. He nervously tried to sidle past Butch so he could get the hell out of there. Butch grimaced at the man, his rotten teeth adding to his sinister demeanour. The man noticed the blood on Butch's clothes and boots and desperately wished he hadn't. Butch cocked his head to one side. 'Want to see how a real man fucks?'

The man gave a nervous smile. 'Uh, nah, I'm good, mate. I kinda need to get going.' Loretta watched the exchange between the two men with disinterest as she picked at her teeth. 'Butch, baby, you know you gotta pay the goin' rate, just like everyone else, doncha?' Without warning Butch stormed over to Loretta and demanded she kneel on all fours. Loretta shrugged, popped a piece of gum in her mouth that had been stuck to the bedside table and did as Butch asked. In the few seconds it took for Butch to undress from the waist down, the man fled from the unit as fast as he could and kept running until his lungs burned. Once there were a few kilometres between him and Loretta's place he slumped down on a park bench, puffing and wheezing like an old man, putrid sweat stinging at his eyes. He regretted in that moment that he'd gone to Loretta's on foot, but he couldn't leave his car in *that* neighbourhood. It was likely it would be trashed or stolen. *Or it might be seen.*

The man's intuition about the gothic looking freak who'd been at Loretta's that night was not good; the blood stains on his clothes and boots were a dead giveaway that he'd just been involved in a violent act. Every fibre of his being knew the man was a dangerous criminal. He hoped Loretta was alright; he was fond of her in his own warped way. He made a mental note of the man's features, height and build. He had an awful feeling the information would come in handy in the near future. His conscience prickled. *Actually, it would come in handy right now. He could be linked to a number of the heinous crimes that had occurred around these parts recently.* He was filled with dread, however, at the thought that it could come out that he'd frequented the home of a prostitute if he were to speak up. He decided to keep quiet and lay low instead and hope that the situation would take care of itself for now.

Butch was unable to keep his eyes open. It turned out that committing murder, having rough sex and taking illicit drugs made for an exhausting combination of activities. Seconds after his head touched the filthy mattress that took up half of the floor space in his bedroom, he fell into a deep coma-like sleep. As he drifted off, his subconscious mind took him back to his past to revisit buried memories. In his lucid dream state, he went back to a better time, a time when there was still hope for his future. A time where he could have still amounted to something and made someone proud.

Sarah was smiling that genuine warm smile of hers, her long fluffy cardigan swinging as they walked side by side towards the table tennis table. Sarah consistently made the effort to have one-on-one time with him. She'd been there for him like no other. She was the one constant person and positive influence in his life. She really cared about him, even when he was being a nasty shithead to the others. He was never nasty to her, though.

'If you win the game tonight then you might not get the Easter egg I bought for you!' Sarah was laughing, clearly playing with him.

Sarah gave him an Easter egg each year and was the only person who ever did. He would never forget that. She also gave him gifts for his birthday and at Christmas. Sarah went out of her way to understand his needs, wants and desires. She made him feel like he mattered. He'd felt worthy when he was around her, like he was someone with potential. Sarah was the only one who could get him to focus on achievement-based activities. Boy, did his confidence soar when she praised him! There were other youth workers at his placement who cared too, but no one could bond with him like Sarah could. She was his everything. Not that he was ever demonstrative towards her; he didn't know how to show affection. In an ideal world, Jock would be his dad and Sarah would be his mum.

The only thing was that Sarah always went away every Easter with her family. Her absence left a gnawing hole in his heart that only he knew existed. Normally he was okay with her going away because she always came straight back after her holiday each year. But recently she was starting to pull right away from him, from all of them. She was distancing herself. She may have thought her behaviour went by unnoticed, but it was painfully obvious to Butch. He was losing her; she was slipping away, and his heart was beginning to shatter into a million pieces all over again. First his parents, then Kate and now Sarah. They did say bad luck came in threes. He needed to toughen up, to learn to live with loss. No one stuck around in his life; he clearly wasn't deserving of that. Butch felt there were no lovable traits about him and never would be. That was why he'd changed his name to Butch when he left state care. The new title represented the tough guy he needed to become, moving forward.

CHAPTER 14

When the coast was clear Butch went back to see Loretta. A few days had passed since the murders at Port Elliot. Butch was more than a little pissed that the police had not come looking for him yet. He'd been sloppy and hadn't cleaned up after himself after killing the heartbreaker and her father. Surely his DNA was everywhere? But then of course he'd experienced no recent dealings with the police for them to make the connection. That was a miracle in itself. The pigs were hardly going to put two and two together with nothing to go on. He knew his thoughts were becoming extremely muddled and it pissed him off. This only enhanced his fragile lack of self-esteem. On the one hand, Butch didn't want to be caught and receive a consequent prison sentence but on the other hand, he sure as hell wanted the accolades for the murders. After all, the whole point was to gain the recognition he deserved. Maybe he could become part of an organised crime group one day. If he was incarcerated, then at least he'd finally be top dog. He'd be ranked the highest among his type of people, the type who rated life's achievements in a less conventional way than normal people. *I'm a true schizo, whoo-hoo! Who am I gonna be today?*

As usual Loretta's front door was unlocked and Butch tutted disapprovingly. She was easy prey, not just for him but for any of her punters. The thought of doing away with her held no excitement at all, though. There would be no thrill of the chase, so she wasn't at risk around him. Butch laughed at the irony. She was the only person he was intimate with, so he'd only be disadvantaging himself. But he still thought she should lock her front door. There were plenty of other deviants who'd willingly do unspeakable things to her from around this neighbourhood. *Wait – does that mean I care? Nah; only for my own selfish reasons.*

As he let himself in, he considered that Loretta's unit was pretty much the only place he frequented for companionship these days. He'd stopped hanging out with the local dead-beat junkies, even though he still scored from them. Loretta had her own trauma background and he supposed they had that in common. Was that why he came? Butch laughed at the double entendre. That was why he came alright; he paid the going rate too and timed his visits for when his Centrelink payment hit his account. He reckoned that made him a pretty fair guy. Butch let out a manic laugh; he was a funny guy at times.

Loretta sat cross-legged on the lounge in a pair of baggy track pants and a discoloured white singlet. Her arms sported various cigarette burns, some fresher than others. A couple of her regulars were sadistic pricks and got off on physically abusing her. Loretta was numb to just about everything. The skinny blonde girl was there in person, but her spirit had long gone to somewhere far away.

Loretta was munching a bowl of Rice Krispies and milk was spilling over one side of the bowl due to her unsteady hands.

'Hey Loretta, you really need to keep the front door locked. It's not safe around here!' Butch chided her as he made himself at home.

Loretta glanced at Butch with glassy eyes, seemingly unperturbed that he kept turning up uninvited. Loretta didn't speak; instead she simply patted the space beside her on the sofa. This was how misfits looked after each other. Loretta was glued to the news story on the television despite being too stoned to take it in.

Butch let the lecture about the front door slide. He knew it was a waste of time trying to get through to her. He sank down beside her on the tattered sofa. He was in no rush and could wait for sex. If Loretta needed to eat first to keep her energy up, then it was fine by him. There was nowhere else to be today. Loretta merely switched the television on for company; she was too out of it to follow what was going on. Butch's eyes flickered to the attractive blonde newsreader on the screen who spoke in a serious tone.

'Police are continuing with enquiries into the murders of Paul Henderson and his daughter Jessica Henderson at Port Elliot and are calling on members of the public to....'

Butch leapt up. 'What the fuck?' he screamed.

Startled, Loretta jerked and tipped the remainder of her bowl of cereal straight into her lap. 'Fuck's sake, dude, what's ya problem? You been smoking some weird shit again?' Loretta got up to get a cloth from the kitchenette to clean up the spillage. By the time she came back through to the lounge, Butch had disappeared, and she heard the fly screen slam shut on his way out. Loretta shrugged nonchalantly. She fancied having a day off anyway.

Butch stormed around the block several times, staring blindly into space. A young mother with a toddler in a stroller quickly moved out of his way as he charged past her, forcing her to move onto the busy road to avoid him on the narrow pavement. A car tooted and swerved, narrowly missing the woman and child. The woman's legs turned to jelly while her child remained oblivious. Butch did not register anything going on around him as he marched forward at a frantic pace. All he could think about was that he'd been off his tits on drugs when he'd committed the murders. He was a fucking amateur, a useless prick.

So it turned out it wasn't even the heartbreaker he'd killed; it was her sister! He remembered now that the heartbreaker used to tell him people thought she and her sister Jessica were twins, although he'd never seen them together to compare their likeness. So much for his well-thought-out plan! Butch palm-slapped his forehead and yelled

'Fuck!', causing an elderly man to gingerly trot over to the other side of the road to avoid him.

Just hours before the murders, he'd seen the heartbreaker in her car wearing that stupid orange cardigan she'd begun wearing before she exited from his life. The one he'd caught a whiff of her perfume from, on certain occasions. The one he'd secretly wanted to snuggle into if only she'd been allowed to hug his affection-starved body. *The one she'd clearly loaned to her fucking sister*. The feelings of self-loathing engulfed him as he headed back to the shit hole of a unit that he lived in. Butch felt it was time to suck on the good old ice pipe again. Oblivion was the name of the game.

Butch felt himself slipping into the throes of a deep cloud of depression. He was not for staying on this earth for too long if he could help it. But he would damn well die as a 'somebody' and go out in style. He wanted his name mentioned for years to come in relation to the heinous crimes he'd committed. He'd often been envious when watching documentaries on serial killers. Ted Bundy was a *bad* motherfucker, yet he was better known globally than most pop stars. Go figure. You didn't have to do something good to be widely recognised, you just had to do *something* significant that affected the lives of others. *Preferably in a bad way.*

Butch pondered on those who'd wronged him and felt certain that his mission here on earth was to rid the world of them. For the benefit of future kids growing up in care, the world needed to know what that felt like and why messing with one's emotions was not recommended.

Butch sat up straight, suddenly feeling a sense of renewed energy. This whole mission was far from over! There were actually two heartbreakers on his hit list, but he'd targeted the main one first. *The one who hurt me the most.* So what if it turned out that he'd killed the sister of heartbreaker number one by mistake. It was merely a case of mistaken identity. *Well in that case, that murder could count as a practice shot to gear up for the real deal!* Butch suddenly leapt up and screamed with laughter. *With heartbreaker number two, there was no chance of her identity being mistaken for someone else though, no siree!*

Butch decided to write a new riddle and post it to the local police station.

Riddle me this:
First there was one heartbreaker
And then there were two.
Both still alive by default for now,
Whoo-hoo!

Riddle me this:
If I count the sister
Then there are three.
What a trip
This is turning out to be!

CHAPTER 15

Kate Jones was an attractive brunette, tall and slim with high cheekbones and large hazel eyes. She stretched out on her sofa, her long legs crossed, her hands clasped around a steaming mug of tea. Her eyes clouded over, and she shuddered at the story being relayed on the news segment on channel nine. The story was about the recent murder of a young woman and her father in Port Elliot. The family were staying in a holiday rental home for the Easter weekend when an intruder broke in and randomly killed two innocent people for no apparent reason. There seemed to be no obvious motive and thus far, the killer was still on the loose.

Sadly, it was not an uncommon theme these days and such stories caused less outrage from the general public than they used to. The story prickled at something in her subconscious. The news segment was a stark reminder of the horrific things she'd witnessed next door all those years ago. Kate shuddered; it was still completely surreal that the little boy living there had witnessed his father killing his mother right there in the family kitchen. He'd been taken into the care of the state at the time. Kate was no psychologist, but she knew that the impact on the boy was enormous and as a result it was more than likely that he'd become a highly traumatised young man. Kate often wondered where he was now and what he was up to.

Kate reflected on all the times she'd noticed that he was home alone. She'd only been nineteen herself; just a kid trying to suss out how to live independently. Once she'd gained his trust, they'd chatted more frequently over the small fence separating their houses. Kate wasn't overly maternal, but she'd felt for the boy, often feeding him, bringing him crappy little toys from Cheap as Chips and offering him her company, even when she really didn't feel like it. Sometimes he would come over and sit on the front step with her to pass the time until his parents came back from the pub.

As Kate's thoughts returned to the present, she noticed a tremor in her hand as she curled her finger through the handle on her mug of tea to raise it to her lips. It was a sure sign that the news segment was triggering her. She reached for the television remote control to turn it off. Her playlist on Spotify would be a much better option to listen to. But the unwelcome thoughts started to creep back in as she dwelled on the past. Kate's thoughts whirled in an unhealthy cycle of guilt followed by justification of her actions.

I should have done more at the time. Maybe I could have prevented what happened to that kid. But the police and child protection services were never privy to what I saw. They couldn't act without concrete evidence. They never got to see the extent of what went on; it was such a messed-up situation. By the time he was taken into care, the damage was done. I should have let him come here for more respite visits than I did. I was young and selfish and put my needs before his. But he was not my responsibility either!

Kate had not moved from her Enfield home following the murder next door. Her friends found it odd that she could remain living beside the house where such a brutal crime had taken place. But Kate felt an obligation to maintain a bit of normality for the child involved. After all, her home was the one and only place he could visit that was familiar. If she took that away, he would have nothing to relate to, once he left residential care and was back on the outside. The little boy had been obsessed with Kate's garden gnome that stood on her front porch. Half of its left arm was missing but she couldn't part with it. Like her, the boy also seemed to identify with its brokenness and somehow it brought comfort to them both. *It will have to be on his terms if he wants to take a trip down memory lane and come back here to see me.*

As Kate pondered about him, she wondered how he was faring in life and tried to push down the unwelcome stirrings of guilt again. The truth was, her feelings about him were mixed. The poor kid had had no one in his life other than her and she was only in it by default, due to the proximity to his family while he was being abused and neglected. Kate shuddered as the memories of the crime scene came flooding back. An unwelcome vision popped into her head of the house next door being cordoned off while police swarmed all over it, with the media camped out in front, their incessant flash bulbs capturing every movement. She'd been scared to leave the house at the time and ended up jumping over her back fence to throw the journalists off the scent. She showed no interest whatsoever of appearing on television with a microphone shoved in her face. She'd never understood people who got off on drama and sensationalism during tragedies.

Strangely enough, no one had lived in the rental home next door for more than a few months ever since. Kate often wondered if the place was haunted by the woman who had been murdered there. She'd suggested to the last tenants that they try to clear the negative energy by burning sage incense sticks in each room, but they'd just looked at her as though she had two heads. Presently a Sudanese family were living there. They'd only moved in a couple of weeks ago, but she would not be surprised if they too broke their tenancy after a short time.

Kate was the only living soul the boy had a valid connection with outside of his residential care home. Kate often felt the weight of this burden on her conscience. The situation was a bone of contention for someone like Kate, who was admittedly self-centred. At the time of the boy's removal, a social worker had approached her and asked if she was interested in being assessed as a potential carer for him in case the kinship options they were scoping did not eventuate. Kate tossed and turned for a couple of nights while considering it. In the end she'd decided that she would compromise and offer occasional respite care on weekends. The arrangement was easy while he was young, as he was easily pacified by watching *Batman* DVDs, but as he grew older, she'd find him staring blankly into space long after the movie had finished. She recalled finding it odd that he often sided with the villain rather than the hero, but maybe it was down to his upbringing. The poor kid hadn't exactly been provided with any positive role models. *Not that I experienced that privilege either and I turned out okay. We can make choices in life; certain people just choose to stay in victim mode forever.*

The kid was initially placed with his auntie, but the placement broke down and he ended up living in residential care with a group of other young people. Kate was relieved at the time, naively thinking that this was the best place for him. She'd assumed that he'd thrive amongst his peers in such a setting. But on the odd weekend when she'd had him over for respite care, he'd told her how diabolical it was. *Yet I still didn't offer to take him in full time. I'd never have shunned him completely though. Providing occasional respite care is better than providing none at all, right?*

Kate felt certain that he would come to see her at some point now that he was an adult. Kate reflected that it was kind of strange that he hadn't appeared up to now, though. Perhaps she could reconcile her feelings of guilt then, and make it up to him somehow. It was weird how the respite visits had ended abruptly back then. When she'd rung up Woodies to ask about it, the staff wouldn't give much away. Kate had just assumed that the boy was no longer fussy about seeing her. But all the same, it didn't sit well with her as she knew he enjoyed her company. *Maybe I gave the poor kid mixed messages because I wasn't consistent with how often I saw him?*

Given the confidentiality around children in care, she'd figured that it was probably pointless trying to ascertain the reasons she no longer saw the boy and consequently cancelled her carer registration. Her carer payments ceased not long afterwards but she'd never been in it for the money. The payments had been sporadic, so it wasn't as though she'd factored them in as regular income.

Kate assumed that the state government must have found him a decent independent living option since he'd surprisingly not been forthcoming in visiting her since he had left care. As her conscience continued to prickle about the fact that she hadn't seen him for a long time, she could only hope he was safe and well. Kate envisaged that if he came to see her, he'd stand transfixed, staring at that kooky gnome on her porch just like he always had as a small kid while passing the time until his mum and dad came home. Maybe she had more in common with the boy than she cared to realise. Kate did not have much to do with her own nutty family, so in a sense she understood his identity issues and feelings of not belonging anywhere.

Kate stood up to put her mug in the sink. Forcing herself to shelve her thoughts about the boy, she turned her mind towards picking an outfit for her latest Tinder date. She prayed that Scott would be just as he had portrayed himself online. Despite the recent influx of creepy poems being placed in her mailbox, she was not following the advice that Detective Dylan Mathews had given her. He'd asked her to lay low on the dating scene and if possible, to live elsewhere, or at least have someone stay with her until the police had investigated who her stalker might be.

Kate was both naive and stubborn and given she was only in her early thirties, she was not about to put her life on hold based on the advice of some flabby middle-aged cop. She was more freaked out by the poems than she would care to admit, but she'd be damned if she was going to stay in every Saturday night when she wasn't getting any younger. Kate wracked her brains about the writer of the poems and at first, she'd drawn a blank. But recently she'd felt an inkling that it was Tom, whom she'd dated briefly. She'd found out he wasn't even eighteen years old yet and had promptly ditched him. He'd looked way older than his tender years, but she'd been suspicious about his lack of maturity and ended it after a couple of dates. Tom presented with a fragile ego and hadn't taken too kindly to her rejection. Kate reckoned he was harmless enough and was probably just suffering from hurt pride. She'd given his details to the police, along with the names of a few other men she'd dated recently. She knew the police intended to question Tom and she hoped that would be the end of it. As soon as the idiot realised he'd been busted, he'd stop trying to intimidate her and move the hell on. The more she thought about it, the more certain she became that Tom was the culprit and her fear began to diminish a little. *He is just a silly little boy trapped in a man's body and needs to grow the hell up! Detective Mathews will soon sort him out!*

Kate knew deep down that she was giving herself a pep talk to convince herself that she wasn't in any current danger. She simply could not allow her brain to compute that there was any more to the creepy poems than a young bloke feeling hard done by that she'd rejected him. In an attempt to take her mind off the uneasy tight feeling that sneaked its way into the pit of her stomach, she turned her thoughts back to tonight's date. *I already know that Scott looks too good to be true, but my need to overcome my incessant loneliness always takes over any rational thought process in the end.*

Kate took a long shower, then selected a short pastel-coloured floral dress from her wardrobe and a pair of high-heeled denim wedge sandals. As she slipped the dress over her new cream silk underwear, she shuddered with anticipation at the thought of Scott taking her dress off her, later.

No! I should really listen to the advice given by the police and stop bringing blokes back here! I can't let being horny cloud my judgement if it affects my safety!

As Kate puckered her lips to apply her pillar-box red Mac lipstick, she knew she wasn't fooling anyone, least of all herself. If Scott wanted her, he'd have her. She was craving sex like there was no tomorrow. Maybe she was ovulating, and her body was crying out to make a baby. She chuckled softly at the thought. She checked the time on her mobile phone and noted there was just under an hour until Scott picked her up from her place. She knew it was a risk to give out her address, but it was either that or make her own way to Glenelg, and she'd decided it was all too hard. The public transport options were dire; there were no direct bus routes near her house, and she could not afford to keep using Uber cars.

The idea for tonight was to become acquainted over dinner and drinks and see where the evening took them. As Kate applied the finishing touches to her make-up, she stood up and smoothed down her dress. She glanced at her nervous expression in the mirror and experienced an unwelcome flurry of butterflies. A film of sweat started to bead on her upper lip. Muttering obscenities under her breath, she wandered back through to the kitchen and hastily poured a large glass of Giesen wine. She glugged down half the glass greedily in one go, feeling annoyed that she still felt the need for Dutch courage despite how many times she'd done this dating thing.

A sharp unexpected knock at the front door caught Kate off guard and she gave a small yelp as she jumped in fright. *Gosh, I really do have the jitters today! Scott is keen! He is way too bloody early; I haven't even blow-dried my hair yet! Thank god I'm looking presentable otherwise!*

Kate teetered unsteadily down the hallway to greet her date. *Maybe these heels are a bit too high. I might have to change into my black sandals instead.*

As she opened the front door and her brain registered who her visitor was, her eyes widened, and she gave an uncertain half smile. Her visitor cocked his head to one side.

'Well, hello there! Aren't you looking pretty!'

Kate stepped back uncertainly, confusion etched on her face. Was he smiling or grimacing? The hairs stood up on the back of her neck as her intuition provided the answer she was looking for. Instinctively, she went to push the front door shut but her visitor was quick to wedge his booted foot inside the door frame before she could do so.

'Now, now, Kate, that's not a very nice way to greet me, is it?'

Kate attempted to speak but a strangled noise came out instead. The look in his blank grey eyes was terrifying. At that point, Kate's visitor punched her in the face so hard that she flew backwards down the hallway with alarming speed. She was instantly knocked unconscious as her skull connected with the wooden floorboards.

CHAPTER 16

Dylan jerked awake as his on-call phone vibrated mercilessly on his bedside table. Squinting at the time, he noted it was 5.00am as he grunted to his boss that he was all ears. Marie stirred restlessly and pulled the duvet up over her head while muttering obscenities. Even though she'd been subjected to her husband receiving calls at an unearthly hour for several years now, she was still mighty pissed off every time his phone rang. Either of them could have slept in the spare room, but neither wanted to give up the comfort of their plush king bed with the feather duvet that had cost them a small fortune. As Dylan grabbed his dressing gown and trundled out of the bedroom, Marie stretched out in a star shape and prayed she would get back to sleep so that she would not feel like a raging menopausal psycho when she faced her colleagues at work in a few hours.

Detective Senior Sergeant Robert Gardner quickly filled Dylan in on the gruesome findings by a hysterical member of the public named Jemma Forbes. Jemma had advised in her statement to police that she suffered with insomnia so she'd taken her golden retriever Benjy for a walk in the early hours to try and tire herself out. Jemma figured that traffic and people would be scarce, around that time. So she kept her dog off the lead as he was generally obedient. Jemma stated that she had walked a few blocks and was about to head home when Benjy suddenly bolted into someone's front garden and cocked his leg to pee. Jemma scolded her dog and lurched forwards to try and grab him by the collar to steer him away from the property. Benjy ignored Jemma and ran up to the front door of the house, which was ajar. Jemma explained she'd hesitated, wondering if perhaps an elderly person lived there and had forgotten to lock the door, or worse still, maybe someone was waiting to pounce. Jemma described a feeling of foreboding. The porch light came on due to the sensor and Jemma noticed a creepy-looking garden gnome with half of its left arm missing. She'd shuddered, recalling that she had felt a chill run down her spine as she edged closer. Jemma said it was odd that Benjy was being disobedient. She reckoned he was following a scent that had piqued his interest. Jemma tried to grab him by the collar again and tripped up the front step in the process. She automatically put a hand out to break her fall and inadvertently pushed the front door wide open. She looked down the hallway and saw a body lying face down in a pool of blood. Jemma's consequent screams caused half of the street to come out to see what the hell was going on. Ironically, no one in the street had seemed to hear or see anything at the time of the murder, which would prove frustrating for the investigating team.

As Dylan shrugged his jacket on and headed to the murder scene, he wondered if the Riddler was responsible for this gruesome death. His sixth sense gave him a dreadful hunch that he was.

Dylan was seasoned at attending crime scenes, but it never became any easier. This one was particularly harrowing because he felt that his team had failed the victim by not finding her stalker before he killed her. As he'd feared, the victim turned out to be Kate Jones. Sadly, Dylan had intended to assist Kate by setting up hidden cameras around her home that very day. *A day too fucking late!* Although Dylan could kick himself, he realised it was out of his control – that more pressing matters had kept coming up that had prevented him from helping her sooner. Now the poor woman had been brutally murdered. The force of the blows she sustained were evident in the grotesque swelling and bruising all over her limp body.

Her killer had ensured he'd finished the job by shooting her in the chest at close range.

The harrowing scene showed an explosion of blood and flesh splattered all over the walls in the long narrow hallway. The horror depicted there was a gruesome sight that made Dylan inwardly gag but he was able to hide it well, after years of practice. Like others in his field, he'd become accustomed to the vile attack such a scene has on all of the human senses. His face remained impassive, however, and he appeared unaffected due to his well-practiced unreadable expression. Playing the part was a huge aspect of the detective role, although many of his colleagues would never admit their bravado was all an act.

Dylan pondered about the fact that Senior Sergeant Gardner had just told him that a woman had been murdered next door to Kate's property thirteen years earlier. Dylan's intuition told him this was no coincidence and that somehow there was a connection. *But what the hell is it?*

As soon as it was daylight, the crime scene investigators arrived and commenced the grim task of suiting up in preparation to lock down the area. Their role was to painstakingly collect blood, DNA, shoe impressions, cigarette butts and any tiny fibres that might hold vital clues. Once all the key players had done all they could for the time being, Dylan headed back to the police station for a briefing with the rest of the team.

Gardner stood in front of a large whiteboard as he addressed his colleagues with the no-nonsense approach he was renowned for. He looked at the sea of weary faces in front of him then squared his shoulders and straightened his back. This was a habit he'd subconsciously started after becoming a senior sergeant. Dylan secretly thought he was puffing his chest out due to suffering from small man syndrome.

'Okay, so let's recap what we know about our victim so far.' Gardner pointed to a photo of Kate Jones that he'd pinned to the board. The picture was recent; Kate was wearing the same floral dress she'd died in. Her eyes were wide in the image and she was laughing. The image had been retrieved from her mobile phone for the purpose of having a recent photo for the murder investigation. At this point it was unclear who'd taken the photo. Dylan sincerely hoped it hadn't been her killer.

Gardner's eyes swept the room, his tone abrupt. 'Just to recap what we already know. The murder victim is Kate Jones, Caucasian female, thirty-two years of age. She has lived alone since she was nineteen years old. Kate was disconnected from her wider family. We will need to delve into her family history and dig deep. We need to put out the feelers for any family disputes that might be behind the motive'.

Gardner paused for effect, ensuring he maintained a captive audience. 'Kate liked to use dating apps. She had a few close friends and seemed to maintain a small circle.' Gardner nodded at Ben Norris, the newly transferred detective on the team. 'Ben, I want you to follow up with organising the interviews with the extended family members and friends.'

Norris nodded. 'Roger that, boss'.

Gardner looked pointedly at Detective Mathews. His lip curled with contempt as he sneered down at him. 'Dylan, what have you got for us so far?'

Dylan cleared his throat, his mouth suddenly dry. He gave a furtive glance around the room before responding. 'As you all know, the team have been actively following up with the men Kate dated recently in a bid to find out the author of those disturbing poems she was receiving. No leads have eventuated so far but we will obviously be checking all suspects again for alibis following her murder.'

Gardner looked unimpressed with the lack of progress and made a point of giving Dylan a drawn-out dirty look as he continued to address the team. 'It looks like the Riddler wants to play cat and mouse with us. He left a note on the hall table. It's been bagged for forensics, but I took a photo of it.'

Gardner pulled out his phone to retrieve the image of the handwritten rhyme.

Riddle me this:
Kate was like ma sis
Meant to care
But did she dare?

Riddle me this:
What do you know about little miss?
I have a face like a trout
She could still have helped me out.

Riddle me this:
I could have lived in bliss
If she'd chosen me instead
She wouldn't be dead

Riddle me this:
How could I kill her, then give her a kiss?
Can you work it out; it's not too profound?
There is a chance I want to be found.

A hush descended over the room as the team digested the words. The only sound in the room was Gardner's marker pen squeaking against the whiteboard as he wrote the poem in large capitals on the shiny white surface. When he was finished, he turned to face the remaining members of the investigating team.

'Get this riddle etched in your heads, pronto. Memorise it, take a photo of it or write it down – whatever works for you. I want everyone in this room attempting to decipher what the hell it means.'

Gardner nodded at Senior Constable Belinda Brown, who was one of his more experienced team members. 'Belinda, I want you to investigate Kate's work history and talk to the staff and manager there. Ask them if anyone of concern frequented the café when Kate was on shift. I know we've already spoken with most of her colleagues and a few of her recent dates, but we also need to speak to any staff who may have quit within the last twelve months.'

Belinda gave a curt nod. 'Yes, boss!'

Gardner continued delegating various tasks until he'd involved every team member and felt satisfied that every job he could think of to bring them closer to solving the murder was covered.

'Okay, let's move it, guys! I want everyone back here for a 4.00pm briefing. I should have received an update from forensics by then.'

The team dispersed within seconds, each eager to do their bit to solve the latest murder.

CHAPTER 17

Following the afternoon briefing, Senior Sergeant Robert Gardner reflected on the new evidence that had come to light. Forensics had matched the footprints left by the killer at both the Port Elliot and the Enfield murder scenes. His fragile ego was dented somewhat by this revelation as he'd silenced one of his less experienced officers who'd suggested the murders may be connected during the previous team meeting. The Riddler hadn't left a poem at Port Elliot so Gardner had remained unconvinced that it was the same killer and had argued this point. He knew deep down that his way of thinking was rather black and white at times. If he was honest, he simply enjoyed contradicting others by way of exercising his authority over them. When he was continually proved wrong it often came back to bite him in the ass; however, his arrogance and lack of integrity meant he had zero care factor.

Gardner was aware that another riddle had been received by the Holden Hill police station but it was possible that this was merely a sick prank. All the same, forensics were taking fingerprints from the envelope to gather evidence. The killer was either ridiculously sloppy or he desperately wanted the connection to be made. So far, they knew that the boot imprints found at both murder scenes came from size eleven tactical boots with a moulded midsole. The size and pattern of the boot imprints at both scenes were carefully examined and matched to a particular style designed to fit wide feet. This style of boot had a low-profile rubber sole for better traction on all surfaces. The pattern on the sole was quite distinctive. Now they just needed to find out who their owner was. Gardner groaned. If only it was as easy as it looked on the television cop dramas.

Gardner chewed at his cuticles, a nervous habit that had irritated the shit out of his ex-wife, Angela. At least he didn't have to listen to her daily whinging about *that* anymore. As he glanced out of the car window at the passing scenery, Gardner realised he was driving around aimlessly. This was a habit he had, when he wasn't feeling all that keen to head home. Gardner still hadn't accepted that he lived alone now, even though it was coming up to a year since Angela had announced she wanted a divorce.

A sudden unwelcome flashback entered Gardner's mind and he swerved across to the next lane, causing a united honking of angry-sounding car horns all around him. *Shit I need to get a fucking grip of myself!* Gardner loosened his tie, aware of the sticky film of sweat suddenly coating his back. It didn't help that he'd been around his least favourite detective today. Dylan Mathews was a prick. Despite Gardner's seniority, no one seemed to agree with him regarding his opinion of Dylan and it riled him no end. Gardner was usually met with a stony silence whenever he berated the detective and expected the other officers to agree with him. Gardner curled his lip in contempt. *Mathews is popular and I am not. Well, I'm not there to make fucking friends; I'm there to run the show, so screw the lot of them!*

Gardner realised that while driving deep in thought, he'd taken the turn-off to his old street where the family home was, without thinking. This wasn't the first time he'd done this on autopilot. He'd lived there for so many years, it was an ingrained habit. Normally he'd make a hasty U-turn for fear of Angela spotting him, but not tonight. He was in the mood for a fight. He needed someone to take his frustrations out on. As he approached the front door, he began to reach into his pocket for his house key then swiftly remembered Angela had changed the locks.

Feeling highly irritated, Gardner rang the doorbell and stepped back to look around while he waited. He noted a silver Land Cruiser parked in the driveway. *Surely Angela hasn't bought that; it's not her type of car. Maybe she has a visitor. Either way, I'm curious.*

A man answered the door and Gardner was momentarily stunned. Who was this prick standing in the doorway of his family home? They eyeballed each other warily. Gardner used his usual abrupt tone. 'I need to speak with my wife.'

The man stared at him thoughtfully. As both men took each other in, each one noted they were quite physically alike: short and stout with thinning grey hair and a ruddy complexion. It was rather uncanny.

'Angela isn't here. Can I assume you are Robert?'

Gardner gave a curt nod. 'Where is she and who are you?' he snapped.

The man kept his cool but used a stern voice. 'I'm Bob, and I don't think I appreciate your tone, mate. Angela is out to dinner with your daughter at the moment. I will tell her you came by.'

Bob was short for Robert; to add insult to injury, they even had the same bloody name! Gardner reeled at the sting of Bob's words. *Maddison is back in town and hasn't even contacted me… my baby girl and my wife are catching up without me.* The penny finally dropped. They really didn't want him in their lives anymore. Gardner was mortified to feel a lump rise in his throat following this epiphany. He began to lose his cool and gave Bob a direct unfriendly stare. 'Are you shacked up with my wife?'

A look of pity crossed Bob's face. 'That's twice you have referred to her as your wife, mate, but you are actually in the middle of divorce proceedings. Angela wanted to tell you about us but didn't think you were ready to hear it yet. I'm sorry.'

Despite thinking the guy was an absolute asshole, Bob felt a bit of empathy for the pathetic figure of a man in front of him. His initial bravado had disappeared, and he'd gone from ten back down to zero in the space of a few minutes.

Gardner continued to stare at Bob as he digested this new blow to his already fragile ego, his mouth hanging open, and the expression of a deflated petulant child on his face.

Gardner tried to speak but found to his horror that the words were stuck in his throat. Instead, he turned on his heel and walked back to his car, his shoulders slumped forward in defeat. After staring blindly into space for ten minutes, he finally started the engine and drove to the local park to head for the nearest bench. His twenty-six-year-old daughter had been working in Darwin and he'd not seen her in over a year. His girl was back in town and hadn't even been in touch. He leaned forward, his elbows on his thighs, his head cradled in his hands. It hurt beyond belief. What had become of him? *I haven't addressed my addiction. They meant it when they said I had to make a choice between it and my family. But I couldn't do it. I failed, and now have lost them both forever.*

Gardner finally headed to his rented apartment and poured a large tumbler of single malt whisky. He downed it, then poured another. A single tear slid down his cheek. Could he be rehabilitated? He thought not. But drinking whisky was the least of his worries.

CHAPTER 18

Butch simply could not believe it. He'd murdered Kate in cold blood and had walked away from the scene without the hint of a curtain twitching, or the sound of a siren or a police car in sight. Granted, some seriously loud music had been blaring from the house two doors along but surely someone must have heard the gunshot? Was it really that easy to kill and get away with it? If so, then killing could become quite the addiction. *I could have started this a long time ago! But where is the adulation if I don't get caught?*

Butch remained awake the entire night, savouring and reliving every moment of it. The young killer reflected on how it'd been a bittersweet experience. Butch closed his eyes to go over it once more. He was afraid of losing all the glorious details, so he pulled out a tattered notebook from under his mattress and began to write. He might not amount to much in life, but he knew he could write well. The heartbreaker had allowed him to believe in his talent and he'd even come close to entering a song writing contest once. But then she broke him, and he simply didn't care to try and get the recognition anymore. What was the point in achievement-based activities if no one was around to be proud of you? As Butch angrily unpacked that thought, he began to write quickly in long spidery pen strokes.

Kate answered the door, surprise crossing her face, then a look of wariness. My rotten teeth have that effect on most people when I smile. I have the original trout pout. It was disappointing that Kate (my only real childhood friend) tried to shut the door on me. Now that could really have hurt my feelings, if I had any!

I know I'm strong for a wiry guy, but I really didn't expect her to fly down the hallway at such speed when I throat-punched her. It was a little annoying that I knocked her out straightaway because then I had to wait around for her to come to. I thought about tying her up, torturing her and all those things they do in the movies but then I thought, nah, that's a cliché; it's been done before.

So, I stood over her, watching, reminiscing, and waiting to see what would happen next. I like living on the edge. I thought maybe someone would show up and I could have fun scaring them too. But no one came – story of my life! I pulled out the gun, kept it aimed at her chest. I thought about how easy it was to get my hands on that too. I'm starting to think that you can do anything you put your mind to. The universe aligned everything to happen so easily for me. What's meant to be is meant to be. I don't feel remorse; I feel nothing.

After a bit, Kate started to stir and groan a little, her eyelids flickering. I quite liked watching her; it was kind of peaceful, like she was waking up from a deep slumber. Then her phone vibrated on the hall table. She must have laid it there when she went to answer the door. I saw a text pop up on the screen.

'Hey Kate, sorry to bail at such short notice, but I just can't do this tonight. I have some family stuff going on. Hope you understand. Scott x

The prick she was dating was ghosting her! I felt a little outraged on her behalf. She was all dressed up with nowhere to go! I felt angry at the guy and was tempted to send a message back, but I had to keep my eye on the prize. I was coming down from an ice trip, so it surprised me that I wasn't too crazed at this point. I just stood there as though I had all the time in the world.

Finally, Kate's eyes flickered open. Her body was at a twisted angle on the floor and I wondered if she'd broken anything. It's amazing how my feelings kept swinging from sympathy to hatred. Bizarre really. She stared up at me, confusion and terror in those pretty pleading eyes. I reckon she felt badly winded. I recognised the feeling. It happened a lot during my childhood when my parents threw me around. I know what it's like to gasp for air and wonder if it will ever return to your poor empty lungs.

'Why?' she managed to croak. The red mist I've grown to know and love came over me before I could stop it. I wanted to have a level-headed, drawn out conversation with her. I really did. I wanted fucking answers! But something took over me. I swear I'm possessed by Satan or some shit. I laid into her, all the years of hurt, anger and frustration pouring out of every pore in my body.

I could hear myself screaming in a high-pitched voice. 'You left me to fucking rot in residential care! Why couldn't you take me in and bring me up yourself, you selfish whore?' Then I remembered the staff at Woodies saying she'd been ringing up, asking to take me out. But her mum had told me the truth about Kate, so I refused to go. She didn't really want me; she just wanted to mess with my mind!

As I remembered all of this, I smashed into her, pummelling her with my fists and kicking her with my boots. I regret not giving her the chance to answer me – to tell me what a worthless piece of shit I am, how no one could ever want to love or care for me. But I didn't need her to tell me or explain what I already know. Her bitch of a mother had already spelled it out for me back then.

When I realised Kate was dead, I felt even more empty inside than I had thought was ever possible. I hated the part of my personality that had killed her. Then my other persona appeared uninvited and I felt tears slide down my face. I wiped them away angrily. What the fuck! I hadn't cried since my mum died when I was a kid. I don't tend to feel emotional ever. It was like I was having an out-of-body experience. I saw myself go over to her crumpled body and feel a moment of sadness for what was, what could have been and what was no longer ever going to be. I bent over and kissed Kate's swollen battered and bloodied face. I'd wanted to kiss her ever since I was a kid. Not in a sexual way; just like you would kiss an auntie or something. At least I think that's what normal families do, going by the movies.

At this point Kate was unrecognisable, but it felt right because I'd mourned the old Kate a long time ago. This pathetic shell of a woman could not be associated with the real Kate of many moons ago. The one who I know gave a shit about me at one point, because I felt it. I'm not sure when it changed for Kate, but she must have asked her mum to tell me to save her having to face me herself.

I left the poem I'd scribbled for the cops. I can write them pretty quickly when I'm heightened. I was beyond disgusted when I left. Disgusted with my parents, disgusted with Kate for not saving me, disgusted at her date for cancelling (it would have been great karma for the prick to find what I'd left of Kate for him) and disgusted that despite my vile acts, no one had approached Kate's house or called the cops. I even left the front door ajar and my bloody footprints everywhere. I'm mighty pissed off that nothing I do ever seems to get noticed, but that's all about to fucking change!

When I left Kate's, I saw she still had the same old broken gnome on the front porch. For a second, I swear I felt a pang of remorse. We used to sit near that gnome, Kate and me, back when she appeared to care about my wellbeing. I turned back and spat on the gnome. I glanced briefly at my old house next door for a couple of seconds then closed my eyes. It was all I could manage. I suddenly needed to get out of there. I bolted down the street at lightning speed. The rest is blank. I don't remember getting back here. But I did. Now I wait for the aftermath. I still feel fifty-fifty about being busted. I want to be caught and I don't. I don't even know who the fuck I am. Maybe I'm many people. I think one of my personalities is smart and the other is cuckoo!

Butch hadn't written his recount of the Port Elliot murders in his notebook, though. That night hadn't gone the way he'd planned, and he would feel pissed off if he had to read about where he'd gone wrong.

He'd prepared a poem that he'd intended to leave at the crime scene but in his haste to get away before the police arrived, he'd left without planting it. From now on he'd only write about his achievements. He'd certainly write about Sarah's murder afterwards, though. *Oh yes! I'll take great pleasure in writing about it in great detail.*

CHAPTER 19

Kate Jones's funeral was a small private cremation at Enfield Memorial Park. Her mother, half-brother and two aunts attended out of respect, even though they'd all shunned Kate as a young woman for daring to want to get away from them as soon as she was old enough. The family were not even sure who would take delivery of Kate's ashes. It all felt a tad awkward and false, yet all eyes were on them, given the publicity around the unsolved murder. The family put on a caring and loving façade to save face while they were under public scrutiny. The Jones family resented that all Kate had wanted was to live a clean life away from the toxicity of their gambling, drug habits and domestic violence. They'd barely spoken since she'd became independent. They saw her as a traitor, someone who thought she was better than everyone else. The police were swarming all over them asking personal and nosy questions about their relationships, no doubt suspecting one of them was guilty of foul play.

Kate's mother Sandra was a slight woman with a heavily lined face and sunken cheeks. Her mouth was set in a permanent grim line, which did not look out of place at the funeral. Sandra had not been remotely maternal towards her children and this had affected Kate deeply. Consequently, Kate had subconsciously shunned the thought of committing to a relationship and having kids. She was afraid of history repeating itself. She couldn't bear the thought of turning out to be as lousy a parent as Sandra. It was partly why she'd kept her neighbour's kid at arm's length when he was taken into care and been so non-committal about arranging regular respite visits with him. Although she'd been afraid of getting too close, she'd also known deep down that she'd done more for the boy than anyone else, which gave her a little comfort. While she'd been inconsistent, she knew she'd never given up on the kid completely. She also knew deep down that it hadn't been enough.

Kate's three closest friends arrived together at the funeral. They wept silently in a huddle, their shock and bewilderment at her sudden brutal death evident. They were still convinced that one of her recent dates was guilty of writing the poems. Like Kate they'd felt uneasy about the fact that Tom was possessive and struggled to handle rejection. Now they believed he was also guilty of her murder. The trio were putting pressure on the police to make an arrest. Tom had been questioned and released. Dylan was sure he was not the man they were looking for and could not tell Kate's friends what they wanted to hear. Nothing of any substance was picked up during Tom's police interview to indicate he was a suspect. His alibis checked out too. Dylan refrained from having the same discussions over and over with Kate's friends. He realised they were frustrated with the lack of progress. They just wanted answers and they wanted them now.

Dylan hated the fact that he'd been instructed by Gardner to station himself outside the crematorium. The detective felt his presence was invasive during such a personal and tragic moment. However, after his initial observations of the family, he felt less guilty. *Jeez, they look like a real bunch of hard nuts; I wouldn't want to cross Kate's mother.* Dylan pushed his personal opinions to one side in a bid to remain professional and focused on the task at hand instead. He was there to quietly observe the comings and goings at the funeral, given that the stalker had alluded to turning up there in one of his poems. He desperately wanted to provide a lead for Gardner, who'd been on his case night and day to come up with a suspect. Dylan regularly fantasised about punching his bully of a boss in the face.

The situation wouldn't be so bad if he were being chastised for valid reasons, but the whole team knew Dylan worked his ass off in an attempt to solve the cases he was assigned to. He might be jaded but he was still invested in his job and was a damn good detective. He'd never receive any recognition from Gardner, though. Pigs would fly before that would ever happen and Dylan tried to accept he was unable to change the situation.

A discreet police and media presence was located outside the funeral, however Sandra made it clear they were not welcome to come anywhere near her home, which was where the refreshments and celebration of Kate's life were to take place. Upon arriving at Sandra's house, two other male guests appeared. One was Kate's boss from the café she'd worked at and the other was a tall lone figure wearing a black hooded sweater which was covering most of his face. He was carrying a tray of sandwiches and as he slid behind Kate's friends, they didn't pay him much attention, assuming he must have been hired from a catering company. When they mentioned this person to Kate's family later, no one knew who they were talking about. The identity of the hooded figure remained a mystery. The young man had disappeared not long after he'd arrived.

The killer wasn't dumb enough to go to the crematorium. But he'd attended the wake, just as he'd threatened in the poems. He'd hoped Sandra would recognise him; would welcome him even. But the bitch hadn't even noticed his presence, even though he'd transported the soggy-looking sandwiches from the kitchen to the lounge to get her attention. The family members had been deep in conversation and not one of them had looked his way. Kate's pathetic friends had noticed him initially, but showed only a fleeting interest. He'd made no impact at all! Furious, he'd retreated in disgust. He'd never made a grand entrance, not even during his birth. He was Mr Nobody. *Split personalities are so much fun! I wanna be caught; I don't wanna be caught. Which is it today?*

CHAPTER 20

Dylan disliked continually probing family and friends for more information when the funeral was still so fresh in their minds. But he was frustrated beyond belief that no significant breakthrough had come through for either the Port Elliot or Enfield murder cases, despite accumulating many vital clues and evidence. They had the bastard's footprints and what was potentially the killer's saliva had been collected from the gnome on Kate's front porch. They just needed to match it to someone's DNA pretty damn soon. The statements taken from the neighbours at both murder scenes proved fruitless. Other than hearing gunshots, no one at Port Elliot had seen the killer's movements. Dylan found it difficult to believe that not a single neighbour had reported hearing or seeing anything at the Enfield murder. At least not until that poor young woman had come across Kate's body and screamed the entire neighbourhood down.

Dylan's thoughts continuously flitted between the Jones, Henderson and Whitaker families. Sarah Whitaker's family had provided extensive information about their colleagues, friends and relatives in a desperate bid to find Paul and Jessica's killer but nothing glaringly obvious stood out to warrant a murder motive. At this stage, it was still unclear if it was a random attack or not. It left Dylan scratching his head in frustration.

Dylan found it odd that none of Kate's family, friends or colleagues provided any real information of substance to assist with his enquiries. Going by current findings, a definite link existed between the Port Elliot and Enfield murders but what exactly was the connection and why had the Riddler not left a poem at the Port Elliot murder scene, if that was his modus operandi?

At least Senior Constable Ben Norris was on secondment to his team, thanks to his recent transfer request being approved. Coincidently, Norris had been first on the scene at the Port Elliot murders and had provided vital information about the case, unlike Ben's previous sergeant, who was being rather uncooperative. Ben's old boss had an issue with working across the two separate police districts to solve the murders, despite the increasing evidence indicating they were connected. Often, Dylan's calls were left unreturned. *I get the message loud and clear. You want me to work my patch and you to work yours. Well it doesn't work like that when cases are linked, asshole!*

After the third round of unsuccessful interviews with all of Kate's close connections, one of her friends, Nadia, finally called Dylan to mention the stranger at the wake. Nadia said it had just occurred to her that this person seemed to be there one minute and gone the next. Kate's friend gave a description of a young man in his early twenties, around six feet tall, with a lanky build and a hood covering his face. No one seemed to know who this person was and no one had interacted with him. Not one person at the wake recalled a person of this description arriving or leaving. The young man was only spotted briefly while carrying a tray of sandwiches. The lack of concrete information was frustrating and provided little substance to form a solid lead. Dylan felt as though he were back on the road to nowhere.

Dylan flipped up the paperwork on his desk in frustration. As he picked up the scattered papers, he felt angry that he hadn't heard about the stranger at the wake sooner. He wondered if Kate's killer had been lurking among the funeral guests, as threatened in his poems, after all. Dylan mentally went through everyone who'd been interviewed by police for the umpteenth time. He frowned as he thought about Kate's mother. Sandra was an odd character, for sure. He'd never seen anyone so unperturbed about losing their daughter. *Perhaps a little more digging into the Jones family dynamics was required.*

Dylan returned to the room at the police station where they held their briefings. He stood with his hands on his hips, his eyes narrowed, while contemplating the information gathered so far. All the clues and evidence collected up until now were pinned to the white board. There were copies of the poems, the identikit of the suspect and the matching footprints at both murder scenes. Dylan stared again at the photo of Kate, which was pinned to the top of the board. *I have an awful feeling that the killer is obvious and there is something I'm missing or not taking into consideration. Am I covering all bases?*

Feeling defeated he trudged back to his office, his head stooped while deep in thought.

Belinda marched towards him, waving her arms to get his attention. 'Boss, Sandra Jones is at the front counter. She says she has rather important information to give you.'

Dylan immediately perked up. 'Send her straight in to see me, thanks.'

Sandra appeared a few minutes later, looking dishevelled. Dylan waved Kate's mother over to the chair on the other side of his desk. He still did not get the vibe that she was a woman who was grieving the loss of her daughter; however, he accepted that not everyone was capable of displaying emotion and people were entitled to grieve in different ways.

Dylan gave a weak smile. 'Please, sit down. What can I do for you today?'

Sandra sucked her cheeks in, contemplating her reply. 'I've been thinking about the kid that Nadia claims snuck into my house for the wake after Kate's funeral.' Sandra paused.

Dylan gave an encouraging and somewhat impatient nod. 'Yes, what about him?'

Sandra chewed at her cuticles and Dylan could not help but notice her finger nails were filthy.

'Well I didn't see him, so he must've been in and out of my house really quickly. But when Kate's mate Nadia described him to me later, it made me think it might be the kid who used to live next door to Kate when he was a young boy. He ended up in care, but would be an adult now.'

Dylan sat up straight in his chair, his eyes glued to Sandra's. 'Go on,' he said in a friendly tone.

Sandra sighed. Her conscience prickled as she remembered the cruel and untruthful words she'd said to the young boy all those years ago.

Dylan's face gave nothing away as he gave his best encouraging nod. Sandra ran her tongue over her teeth as she thought of what she should say next.

'This kid; he knew where I lived. When Kate used to have him at her place for respite care, they used to pass our place when they walked to the local shops. When I was sitting out the front one day, she introduced me as her mum. It was kinda awkward, ya know? Because we didn't see eye to eye after she'd left home. But I was nice for the kid's sake.'

Dylan nodded, thinking that Sandra seemed anything but nice. Sandra gave him her best sheepish grin.

'Look, I admit now that when you showed the family a copy of the poem left by Kate's killer to ask if it meant anything to us, I had a hunch at the time who might be responsible for my daughter's death.'

Dylan raised a questioning eyebrow, noticing her hesitancy in continuing with her confession. Sandra ran a trembling hand through her short, brittle dyed blonde hair.

'At first I pushed the thoughts away. It was easier to bury my head in the sand, ya know? But the words of the riddle began to haunt me whenever I tried to sleep at night. I couldn't fight it anymore; I had to let you know. For my Kate's sake. God rest her soul. Every time I shut my eyes, the words of the Riddler dance in front of me.'

Sandra shuddered. She could still see the words in her mind's eye; she'd read over them enough.

Riddle me this:
Kate was like ma sis
Meant to care
But did she dare?

Riddle me this:
What do you know about little miss?
I have a face like a trout
She could still have helped me out.

Riddle me this:
I could have lived in bliss
If she'd chosen me instead
She wouldn't be dead

Riddle me this:
How could I kill her, then give her a kiss?
Can you work it out; it's not too profound?
There is a chance I want to be found.

Dylan tried to hide his irritation at the delay in Sandra parting with the information she'd come to divulge. She looked like the proverbial deer caught in the headlights. Given half the chance, he was sure she'd bolt out of his office as fast as she could. *Is getting this off her chest at this late stage really to help with our police enquiries or was it just a way of dumping her pent-up guilt elsewhere in a bid to get rid of it? Guilty conscience, or what?*

Sandra peered at him through her sunken hooded eyes. She paused uncertainly, then decided to go on.

'Look, I'm not proud of it, but I told the kid one day that Kate didn't want to let him come to her place for respite care anymore. There is every chance he held a grudge against her for it. Kate never knew that I'd said that to him. Anyhow, my cousin Rhona reckons she lives in the same housing unit block as him now. He has grown all tall and lanky and the locals call him Butch. Rhona probably wouldn't have put two and two together but sometimes the wrong mail gets placed in her mailbox. So, she got to know the kid's name when she got his mail by mistake and well… it's the same name as that kid who used to go to Kate's for respite visits: Shaun Wallace. His dad murdered his mum; it was all over the news back in the day. You'd know the case.'

Sandra bowed her head and lowered her gaze as she waited for her words to sink in.

Dylan felt enveloped in a strange mix of rage at the lateness of this vital news and euphoria that he might finally have the breakthrough he so badly needed. Sandra could sense his annoyance; his jaw tightened and he was staring at her through critical eyes, his mouth set in a grim line. She began talking at a rapid pace.

'Look, me 'n' Kate, we weren't close. She took off when she was quite young to do her own thing, ya know?'

Sandra's eyes unexpectedly became glassy with tears, which she quickly blinked away. Showing any emotion was a weakness, where she came from.

'I didn't do the right thing by my girl, alright? I'm owning up to it now cos I've been a harsh mum, but this has been playing on my mind a bit.'

Sandra shrugged, her watery blue eyes full of long-overdue regret. As if to justify what she'd said to the boy, she added an afterthought. 'I thought Kate was in it for the money, ya know? She wasn't sharing her carer payments with the rest of us, so I tried to get back at her by putting the kid off from coming. I was a crazy bitch for doing that. As soon as I saw how crushed he looked, I knew I should never have said it. But I couldn't unsay it and I never did anything to put it right. That's why I'm here now.'

Sandra stared pleadingly at the detective, whose face remained stony. The woman was desperate for praise. Dylan guessed that her own childhood had probably been as messed up as Kate's. This sad figure of a woman was more than likely a kid trapped in a middle-aged body with several unresolved issues. There were too many of these people around not getting the help they needed and all the while continuing the cycle of messing up their own kids' lives. Poor Kate; she had fared the worst. Dylan let out a long sigh. The situation was all kinds of tragic.

Dylan softened a little as he surmised that Sandra was at least attempting to put things right, albeit in her own warped way. Finally, he said the words she so badly wanted to hear. 'You've done the right thing telling me all of this. It is crucial information that we need, to continue with our enquiries. Now I will need you to take part in a formal recorded interview. Can you do this now?'

Sandra nodded, with a look of apprehension. Dylan waved down Belinda, who was walking down the corridor past his large glass office window. He popped his head around the office door.

'Can you take Ms Jones to interview room three, please? She has important information which may assist in locating her daughter's killer.'

As he watched Sandra follow Belinda down the corridor, he shook his head in disbelief. *That woman is as cold as ice. I wonder what her own story is? I will leave that one to the quacks; I have enough mysteries to solve....*

CHAPTER 21

Sarah opened her eyes and stared at a hairline crack in the ceiling. Almost immediately the nightmare of the last two weeks came flooding back in glorious technicolour. She'd suffered constant sleep disturbances and nightmares, following the deaths of her dad and sister. Sarah couldn't see how her current state of mind would ever change. At that moment she felt that her grief would surely engulf her forevermore. She was trying so hard to be the pillar of strength that the family needed right now. Her poor mum was falling apart, and Sarah was dismayed to feel like she was following suit. She glanced at Nick's sleeping form beside her and felt a red-hot anger rise in her chest. *How can he sleep? How can any of us sleep ever again?*

Sarah knew deep down that her thoughts were irrational. Her poor husband was probably only sleeping due to sheer exhaustion. Nick had chosen the rental house where the murders had taken place. He felt partly responsible for the deaths of his father-in-law and sister-in-law, despite knowing it was crazy to blame himself. But despite reassurance from Sarah's mum that he was not to blame, the same thoughts plagued him and played mercilessly on repeat in his head.

Sarah wouldn't admit it, but she was having similar thoughts. *Does the fact that Nick chose the holiday rental make it his fault that my dad and sister were shot and killed by a psychopath who remains on the loose? Of course not, but I still feel angry with him! I just want to rewind that weekend and never leave Adelaide. I want justice and can't rest until I get it. I need to take my anger out on someone and it's making me feel insane!*

Despite the breadth of her education, Sarah could not stop any of the irrational thoughts she was having. Feeling weary before the day had even begun, she wandered through to the kitchen, the ever-present tightness in her forehead, throat and chest. She clawed wildly at her neck in a fit of despair. *I constantly feel like I'm suffocating.*

With trembling hands, Sarah poured a glass of water and took a few tentative sips; however, it did nothing to alleviate her parched mouth. The dreaded hollow feeling in her stomach reappeared and waves of nausea swept through her. *I have to get a grip; I have to face what's happened. I need to remain strong for my mum, Nick and Finn. Most of all, I need to seek justice for my dad and Jessica. But I feel claustrophobic in my own body right now. I don't want to face this nightmare every day. But I have no choice.*

Sarah felt the familiar feeling of panic rise through her body and began to hyperventilate, her breath coming in short bursts as she struggled to inhale the oxygen she so badly needed. Nick appeared at her side, the black rings under his eyes telling a story of their own. Nick led his fragile-looking wife out to the back yard for fresh air. He sat beside her on the garden bench and gently encouraged her to go through the breathing exercises the grief and loss counsellor had suggested to them. Nick looked on at Sarah in fear. She'd always been a pillar of strength, so poised and strong when managing the emotions and fears of others. So, to see her like this now, a shadow of her former self, was both terrifying and horrifying. Nick used what he hoped was a convincing, calm tone.

'That's right, honey; take a slow deep breath, in through your nose and then out through your mouth.'

As Sarah responded to Nick's hypnotic tone, her breathing eventually returned to normal and her heart rate slowed. She held on tight to her husband, feeling guilty about her earlier negative thoughts towards him. Nick was her rock and her saving grace. *I need him so badly right now.*

Looking much older than their years, the couple walked slowly back indoors to the kitchen. Sarah watched Nick potter around, going through the motions of making tea and toast. Neither of them really wanted to face eating breakfast but they knew they needed to keep their strength up and maintain a sense of normality. By the time Finn surfaced, they'd composed themselves somewhat for his sake. Finn wasn't fooled by the sad little routine and his parents knew it. Their son was a highly intelligent little boy. Tears pricked at Sarah's eyes as she considered the impact the last few weeks would have had on their son.

Nick ran a hand through his thick black hair and studied his wife's chalk white expression and drawn features. Sarah looked like a shadow of her former self. Being her husband and not knowing how to take her pain away was the worst feeling. The enormity of the situation was becoming too much to bear. They were stuck in the disbelief stage of grief that manifests as an initial numbness, a surreal sense that it could not be happening, that the world around them had stopped making sense.

'I know I say the exact same things every day, but I'm just so worried about my mum.' Sarah's hollow eyes met Nick's. He came and sat next to her and placed his head on her shoulder.

'Your mum is avoiding social interactions because she needs time to process and reflect in solitude for a bit. We know that her post-traumatic stress disorder will be ongoing. I feel so sick thinking about her coming face to face with that fucker. It would have been horrific beyond words.' Nick shuddered at the thought of Jean witnessing Paul being shot. God only knew what his mother-in-law had endured that night. 'Remember, the counsellor told us your mum is likely to dip in and out of grief and will learn to handle it in small doses before regaining emotional control. We just have to give her time.'

Sarah let out a deep sigh to acknowledge Nick's words. She turned to face him, her neck and head rigid with tension. 'We still don't even know the exact details of what my mum witnessed; she just won't talk about that night with me yet. Well, she has to the police, but she is trying to protect me from the gory details. I understand that… but I also need to know exactly what we are dealing with, given that there is a murdering psychopath at large! Everyone seems so convinced it was a random attack with no motive, but we just don't know, do we? Why did the killer bypass our bedroom and kill Dad and Jess, but not Mum? Thank the lord that Finn crawled in for a cuddle that night and was with us! I can't stop thinking about how he started off in my mum and dad's bed before sneaking back into our room.' Sarah paused as she tried to process the events once again. 'None of it makes any sense!' Sarah's voice rose with frustration and anger and she felt instantly guilty as she saw the hopelessness in Nick's eyes.

Finn appeared in the kitchen doorway rubbing his eyes with one hand while clutching his huge brown shaggy teddy bear with the other. The teddy hadn't left his side since their ordeal and it made Sarah's heart restrict as her son stretched his arms out for a reassuring hug, as he approached her. Finn climbed onto his mother's lap and wrapped his tiny arms around her neck. Nick joined them for a group hug, and they stayed that way for several minutes, the two adults each lost in their own tragic thoughts.

CHAPTER 22

Butch was feeling increasingly disgruntled. Why was no one sitting up and taking notice of his capabilities like he'd expected? He knew his mental health was not in a good place. As Butch was now an independent adult, there were no carers to make sure he took the necessary medication for his various mental health disorders. Watching the coverage of the murders was pathetic and he was dismayed to note they were barely even being featured on the news anymore as everyone had moved on to the next big crime. *What the fuck? Why does nothing I do ever matter? Not even murder! Why was I born to be a nobody?*

Butch pulled out a Stanley knife from under his mattress and sliced into the top of his forearm. Cutting himself hurt like hell, but that sweet release of blood was magical, mesmerising even. Self-harm was always the best outlet for his fucked-up feelings. He watched mindlessly as his blood flowed heavily from the wound. Eventually he used a yellow-stained pillowcase to stem the flow. He watched on, fascinated at how quickly the cotton material became saturated with his rich red blood.

Butch reflected on Kate's wake. Nobody had noticed him there either – not even Sandra, Kate's mother – although he had to admit that his visit had been rather fleeting that day. Butch entered a trance-like state as he thought back to the very last time he'd gone to Kate's for respite care.

Kate had taken him to see a *Batman* movie, then they'd gone for dinner. This was around the time that he'd become obsessed with the character named The Riddler. He felt he had a lot in common with the fictional supervillain. Kate had allowed him to come back to her house, where they sat on the porch and drank steaming hot chocolate, which he'd thoroughly enjoyed. All too soon, the familiar toot of a car horn had sounded, indicating that a youth worker was there to pick him up and return him to his residential care placement. It was bittersweet. Life on the outside could be so enjoyable but it was always cut short just in time to head back to the grim reality of living in state care.

They'd said their goodbyes and Kate had gone in and shut her front door. The youth worker had gestured, indicating he was turning the car around to face the way they were headed. As the youth worker concentrated on carefully manoeuvring the government car in a three-point turn, Kate's mother Sandra had suddenly appeared out of nowhere. 'Hey, sonny.'

Butch had stared blankly at the haggard-looking women. After a few seconds, it had registered that the woman was Kate's mum. He'd met her briefly a couple of times when they'd passed by her house on the way to the local shops. He was aware that she and Kate weren't close. She'd confided that to him as a way of making a connection, given his own messed-up family dynamics.

Sandra had clutched at his elbow with a bony hand and he'd resisted the urge to shake her off. She'd peered at him with those cold watery blue eyes.

'I hate to be the bearer of bad news, sonny, but Kate doesn't really want you coming here for respite visits. You know she just feels sorry for you, doncha? But she doesn't really wanna be wasting her weekends with you. She could be out meeting a new boyfriend or something; do you get what I mean? After all, no one wants to be seen with a kid who has a face like a trout!'

Butch's heart felt like it had dropped into his stomach. He didn't have respite visits with Kate as often as he'd like but he'd never got the impression she didn't want him to come at all. Just another rejection. He was too ugly to be seen with. Butch had nodded, his face blank; he had nothing to say. His feet felt like lead with every step he took towards the government car. Slowly a feeling of intense hatred began to build up inside him. Kate would have to pay for this one day. She was a fake bitch just like his mum was.

Sandra had scuttled around the corner to the side street where her cousin Rhona was waiting for her in her car. Sandra clambered into the passenger side, keen to head off in case Kate spotted her in the vicinity. 'I told the kid not to come for visits anymore. We can't be having Kate getting paid carer payments when she won't even share any of it with us! Fuck her! Fuck the kid!'

Rhona nodded and the two women exchanged spiteful glances. Anyone in the family who wasn't up for sharing their money with each other would soon have to pay the price. With a bit of luck, the kid would refuse to come back to Kate's, and she would be royally screwed over when her carer payments stopped. For some reason the family thought the carer payments were much higher than they actually were.

Sandra's mouth formed a tight line as she thought of her daughter. 'I got me a real madam who thinks she is above the rest of the family. She must've only been in it for the money; who else would care about a kid like that? He has a face like a trout!'

Sandra had let out a wicked laugh as Rhona skidded around the corner almost up on two wheels. Maturity was uncommon in the Jones family.

In order for Butch to escape the pain caused by Sandra's words, he had immersed himself in his comic collection, fantasising that he would be chosen to depict The Riddler in any consequent *Batman* movies. He'd decided that, for now, he would have to settle for mimicking his favourite villain by writing riddles to leave as clues for the authorities to solve. Once he'd left care, he knew he would make it happen.

CHAPTER 23

Butch was increasingly restless and needed something to fill his days while he planned out his next move. His unit was filthy with dirty dishes lying everywhere, and smelly unwashed clothes were piled up in a corner. He threw on a pair of old track pants and a hooded top and went out barefoot. Butch walked the short distance to the corner store navigating the broken glass on the pavement, not that he'd really care if he cut his feet. Today was payday and thankfully he was eligible for all sorts of Centrelink payments or he'd be royally screwed. Butch knew he'd never get a job. What would he do? He was useless, always had been, and always would be. *Sarah used to tell me that I was a talented poet and songwriter. But the bitch never stuck around to help me amount to anything in life!*

Butch's eyes narrowed as he walked listlessly around the store throwing any old crap into the wire basket hanging off his skinny arm. He was ambivalent about what he ate. Being healthy and respecting his body wasn't high on his list of priorities. As he stood in line waiting to buy cigarettes, he looked down at his dinner of choice. The basket consisted of a family-sized bag of Doritos and a giant bottle of coke. As the lady at the front of the line was holding up the cashier with her bullshit chit-chat, his thoughts drifted back to a time he'd rather not reflect on, but constantly did.

A few months after Sarah had left Woodies, he'd spotted her at Glenelg. Butch was free to go where he wanted, now that he was of age and no longer under the care of the state. Butch's heart leapt with joy as he quickened his pace and walked towards her. But then he remembered she'd abandoned him, and he stopped dead in his tracks. Wasn't she meant to be living in Melbourne or some shit? She'd clearly lied about that. Butch stared straight at Sarah, waiting for her reaction and willing her to see him. But then his blood turned to ice as she appeared to look straight through him and kept on walking. The bitch sailed right past him as though she'd never set eyes on him in her life. It was as though she'd never even featured in his life! Butch watched her retreating figure as she strolled by and observed her catching up to a man pushing a stroller. Sarah kissed the man, then tickled the child under the chin. The child grinned and cooed up at her adoringly. Butch was no fool. They were obviously her husband and kid. Sarah's departure from his life was starting to make sense. He'd been replaced by the blond brat she was currently fussing over. Butch became consumed with an insane feeling of jealousy as he dry-retched. He honestly thought he might throw up there and then.

That damn red mist came over him again. Butch considered doing away with the brat there and then. After all, he'd harmed a little kid in the past so was more than capable of doing it. But nah, Sarah was the one who'd broken his heart. Sarah was one of two heartbreakers who would pay with their lives for ruining his.

Butch followed the family from a distance, his hoodie pulled up over his head. He even got onto the same tram and sat near them. Still nothing. He'd been in her peripheral vision the whole time, but he may as well have been a ghost.

Sarah snuggled her head on Nick's shoulder during the short tram ride home. 'I'm pretty trashed today, I reckon I had three hours' sleep, if I'm lucky!'

Nick patted his wife's arm. 'Yeah, you are pretty vague today! You are so out of it that you barely even registered Finn and I waving at you when we met up with you just then!'

Sarah gave a weak smile. 'I couldn't be bothered putting my contact lenses in this morning so cut me some slack!'

Nick laughed. 'Thank god the teething stage doesn't last forever; I don't want a zombie for a wife!'

Butch disembarked at their stop and walked a few metres behind them, managing to tail them all the way to their terraced bungalow a couple of streets away. As the young family closed their front door behind them, he gave a menacing smile. Now Butch had something to do with all his free time. He knew where the heartbreaker lived! Over the following weeks, he'd learned all of her routines.

That was when Butch had begun to plan the day of her demise.

CHAPTER 24

Butch could have attempted to kill Sarah a lot sooner than he did, but he knew that half of the fun was the planning and the lead up to it. After all, what would he do once it was all over? Sarah was not his only target, of course, but she was the main one. As far as he was concerned, she was a lying, conniving, disloyal piece of shit who'd led him on for years on end – not in a sexual way, but in the sense that she'd almost had him fooled that she really cared about his wellbeing and his future.

Butch could see now that she had simply just been doing her job as the manager of Woodies. She was a glorified youth worker who'd boosted her ego by appearing as though she was wholly invested in the wellbeing of the messed up young people that she worked with.

Butch was hardened by his life experiences and when he'd been placed at Woodies as a young child, he had never thought he would have allowed himself to have feelings for another person ever again. But Sarah had managed to worm her way into his heart. She'd been insistent, determined to win him over. On reflection, had that been for her benefit or his? Now he truly wondered. Whose needs had she been meeting? Was she massaging her own ego? Was he just some kind of social experiment? If she could walk away from him and the other kids so easily, lie about it and then go off and have a child of her own without letting any of them know, what did that make her? A despicable lying bitch who deserved to die, that's what.

Butch could have taken the whole lot of them out on several occasions but the Port Elliot scenario was way more fun. Butch reflected that it was a pity that Sarah's dumb prick of a dad had got in the way or he could have given the police a good description of him. Maybe he'd be well on his way to receiving his well-deserved accolades by now if the old man had lived to tell the tale. Butch had enjoyed terrorising Sarah's mother. He'd enjoyed seeing her suffer as she looked on helplessly. The old woman could not do a damn thing to stop her beloved husband being shot in the chest. Butch had heard through the grapevine that Sarah's mum had experienced a mental breakdown since her husband was murdered.

Boo fuckin' hoo! How about you tell them something more about the killer other than that he was a tall man wearing a balaclava, so I can become a hero! Can't you remember how god-like I was?

Maybe he should have killed Sarah and her dumb-looking kid when he'd started lurking outside their house back in the early days. *Well I almost did one time.* One night Butch had become rather brazen. Instead of skulking in the shadows after dark like he usually did, he'd walked right into their backyard through the side gate without a care in the world. Sometimes he liked to live on the edge and let fate decide the outcome on any given day. The brat kid was sitting in a high chair at the time and was looking right at him. The kid's eyes were wide with fear, but Sarah had had her back to the glass sliding doors and was oblivious to what her son could see. She was too busy making stupid aeroplane movements with the spoon of food in her hand while pretending to fly the spoon into her son's mouth.

Butch gave the child a menacing smile, his rotten teeth on display. The child screamed and pointed behind Sarah to where Butch was standing outside in the backyard. Butch ducked quickly, taking cover under the outdoor table. By the time Sarah had set down the plate and spoon and turned around to see what was scaring Finn, there was nothing to see. A flock of birds swooped and screeched overhead, and Sarah convinced herself it must have been the ascending birds that had frightened Finn. All the same, she'd felt a prickle of unease and double-checked that the back door was locked.

Butch knew Sarah's husband was away with work that week and it was oh so tempting to do the deed there and then, but his ultimate goal was to kill her when she was away with her extended family. It was all about the impact and the scale of the horror. It needed to be on a wider scale. Butch realised that it was a blessing that he'd been unable to kill Sarah the night he'd followed her to the Bene Bistro. It wasn't meant to be. When he stopped and thought about it, it would be too boring to kill her while alone. The brat kid had been with his grandparents and her husband was working late that night. The beauty of it was that now, he'd enjoyed the luxury of a trial run by accidentally killing her sister. At first, he'd berated himself to high heaven for missing the intended target, but once he'd calmed down, he realised the deliciousness of planning Sarah's murder all over again.

Butch knew from overhearing yet another conversation on the tram that Sarah intended to start going to the Anytime Fitness gym on Shepherds Hill Road with her friend Stacey on Tuesday nights. It was a bit of a drive from her place, but she'd revealed, as she chattered away to her tram buddy, that she didn't mind as she needed 'me time' away from Nick and Finn. As Butch's ears pricked up under his stooped hooded head, he'd formulated a plan. He'd need to borrow Loretta's car again. He smirked as he thought how ironic it was that Sarah had helped him get his driver's licence when he was in care. Now he could finally put it to good use. Butch intended to follow Sarah and suss out the route she'd be taking to go to the gym every week. Butch knew it was quiet around that area, which would be perfect for what he had in mind.

CHAPTER 25

May 2021

Despite the extraordinary efforts made by the police, the killer of Paul and Jessica Henderson, and Kate Jones remained at large. Based on the various sources of information provided by Sandra Jones and others, Shaun Wallace was now a prime suspect. Police were yet to locate him at his home to bring him in for questioning. Shaun Wallace appeared to be missing in action.

Sarah pondered the identikit that had been put together using the description her mum had given of the killer. Given that his face was covered by a balaclava during the invasion, all the police really had to go on was his height and build. This also matched the description given by Kate's friend of the fleeting visitor at the wake. Police were aware of the killer's shoe size and the fact that he had wide feet, going by the imprints left by his boots at both scenes. Sarah was aware that an exhaustive list of friends, family and colleagues had been interviewed but the investigation was yet to yield any results. Sarah was not yet privy to the vital clue provided by Sandra Jones, as she'd been playing phone tag with Detective Dylan Mathews who was trying to get a hold of her.

Sarah needed a break from the relentless torture of reliving that fateful weekend. She decided the best remedy would be to catch up with her good friend and colleague, Jock, who was always happy to lend a listening ear and make her smile. Given that Jock was a jovial and vibrant Scotsman who never failed to make her laugh with his quick wit, she knew he was just what the doctor ordered. Sarah hadn't seen any of the staff from the residential care unit she'd worked at for quite a long time despite being full of good intentions. Becoming a mum had kept her a lot busier than she'd bargained for and the regular catch-ups she'd hoped for with her old team hadn't amounted to much up to now.

It was a hard decision for Sarah not to return to her old place of work. Her maternity leave had flown by and after her heart-wrenching exit, it simply hadn't felt right to go back. Becoming a mother had allowed her to let go of the guilt associated with the feeling that she was letting the residents down because now her priority was her own child. The idea of putting anyone else first was absurd. Upon reflection, Sarah realised how naive she'd been to think that she could leave Woodies without it impacting the young people who lived there as much as it had. For her own wellbeing and peace of mind, she'd opted to work part time in a youth counsellor role in the city, once her maternity leave was up. This meant that she could still help young people in some capacity, but could walk away at the end of her working day and catch a tram home without getting caught up in critical incidents and teen dramas.

The Woodies staff were great at keeping in touch and sent regular messages letting her know that Jock was doing a great job of running the place in her absence. Sarah felt sure they were minimising the aftermath of her departure but also knew it would do her no good to know the truth. Hearing the daily struggles at her old workplace would only make her feel guilty all over again.

Sarah and Nick desperately needed a change of scene, so she was delighted when Jock and his wife agreed to meet them in Hahndorf for lunch. Sarah loved the little town, which was known for its original German-style architecture and artisanal food. Nick's parents offered to take Finn to the beach for the day and Nick and Sarah were grateful for the freedom, given how clingy he'd become. A change of scene would do them all good. They settled for a café with an outdoor dining option so that they could enjoy the early afternoon sun.

As Nick and Kellie both worked in aviation and knew people in common, the conversation between them flowed. Therefore, it was easy for Sarah to slip straight into a conversation about Woodies with Jock. She was always mindful of not talking about residents in front of others, given the confidential nature of their work, so she kept her voice low.

'I hear you are running a tight ship, Jock. I'm also hearing great things about Woodies with you at the helm. The team seems pretty happy having you in charge. Maybe it's just as well I didn't return; I may have had big boots to fill!' Sarah smiled. She felt no envy, only genuine pride and admiration.

'Aye, it seems tae be going well, hen! I huv held back oan tellin' you aboot all the shenanigans that have been going on, though, cos it wid serve nae purpose in stressing ye oot!'

Sarah nodded her head vigorously. 'I agree wholeheartedly! I'm kind of dying to know everything, after being invested in those kids for all these years… but what I don't know doesn't hurt me, right?'

Jock decided not to tell Sarah about the nasty comments the residents had continued to make about her following her departure from the unit. Telling her would serve no purpose and would only hurt her feelings and make her feel worse about leaving than she already did.

Jock nodded thoughtfully. 'I'm not sure if I should tell ye but I saw Shaun Wallace last week. I was helping Beth transition into her independent living accommodation. She moved into the block around the corner fae the housing trust unit that Shaun transitioned into after you left Woodies. Shaun just happened to be walking past on the other side of the road. He wis in a vague dream-like state, like he always is. I almost didnae recognise him. He is looking a bit gothic, all dressed in black with loads of piercings these days. He didnae appear to register that I was there. I was gonnae focus on the task at hand and then call oot tae him to ask how he was getting oan. But then he was naewhere in sight when I turned back roond tae look for him. He looked quite intimidating with his lanky six-foot frame and those big black tactical boots he goes aroond in now. You remember how giant his feet were, right?'

Sarah froze and the blood drained from her face.

'You okay?' Jock looked puzzled; even Sarah's lips were white. She looked like she'd seen a ghost.

Nick sensed the change in the general vibe and glanced over at his wife, his face pinched with anxiety. 'Sarah, what's wrong?' Nick leapt out of his chair to walk over to his wife. He suspected she was going to hyperventilate and experience another panic attack. Sadly, it was becoming a regular occurrence since she'd lost her father and sister.

Sarah looked at Nick fearfully. 'Shit! I have just had an awful hunch that Dad and Jessica's killer is one of the kids I worked with at Woodies. I can't believe I did not consider this before. Am I really that blind and stupid?'

Nick and Jock glanced at each other, confusion etched on their furrowed brows.

Sarah's eyes were wide with fear. 'The evidence gathered by police so far indicates that the killer is around six feet tall, slim build… and has giant feet… exceptionally wide giant feet at that, going by the boot imprints left at the scene of the crime.'

Jock stared at Sarah, his mouth hanging open as the realisation sunk in that she could be onto something. Nick and Kellie looked on, patiently waiting for an explanation; they had no idea what was going on. Sarah was visibly trembling and Kellie placed an arm around her shoulders to steady her. Jock addressed the group in a low whisper.

'We have just cottoned oan tae the fact that there is an ex-Woodies resident whae fits the physical description the police huv o' the killer the police huv nicknamed The Riddler. This Shaun kid has extra-wide feet – we always had trouble finding him shoes he liked – anyhow, he also has a serious trauma background and the medical professionals think he has the markings of a sociopath and the capacity to kill, based on the critical incidents he's been involved in up to now. Now that I say all of that out loud, you would think it would have been obvious. But we are so invested in these kids that we don't ever believe they would go as far as trying to do away with any of us!' Jock shook his head in disbelief. 'I guess we could have been very wrong about that!'

Jock and Sarah's eyes locked as they processed the vital clues they'd clearly missed up until this point. Sarah began to shake, cry and stutter simultaneously as she continued to stare at Jock.

'Holy shit! How could we have overlooked this? The police nicknamed the killer The Riddler because he leaves them poems with clues, and Shaun just happens to be a great lyricist! It's been staring us in the face all along, but we are so used to looking for the good in others that we haven't wanted to believe it was someone we knew, let alone someone we were invested in and cared about! Now I'm starting to think he is definitely connected to the murders!' Sarah's stomach heaved horribly and she began to feel dizzy.

A brief silence followed as everyone digested this information. Sarah pushed her chair back and stood up, her eyes darting wildly as she ran a hand through her chestnut locks. 'How could I have been so naive as to not have thought of this? Shaun would easily have been the kid most affected by my departure from Woodies! I wouldn't be at all surprised if he wanted revenge, to punish me for leaving him!' Sarah began blinking rapidly as her thoughts raced.

'Oh my god!' She slapped a hand across her mouth. 'I think he may have killed my sister thinking she was me! It was a case of mistaken identity! My poor dad probably just got in the way!'

Sarah began to sob as she ran from the café, causing passers-by to stop in their tracks and stare. The others quickly caught up with her and gently steered her over to the nearby park to calm her down.

Once Sarah had composed herself a little, she agreed to go with Nick to the police station to let them know about the pieces she'd finally put together. There was clearly no proof based on hearsay, but it would give them something to go on. Jock and Kellie looked pale and shaken as they drove off, both assuring Sarah that they would do whatever they could to assist the police further with their enquiries.

Sarah stared out of the car window deep in thought as she and Nick drove off in silence. *Surely, I am being neurotic? How could a kid you have done so much for ever want to kill you? Have I been naive in thinking I'd be immune to his hatred of others? Of course he is capable! He consistently ignored the concepts of right and wrong and was harsh, impulsive and violent. He has never shown any remorse for killing those animals or attacking that small boy. Has my ego got in the way of accepting the truth? Was I arrogant enough to think I was untouchable, that maybe I cured him even; that somehow, I'd get a return from my investment in his wellbeing…*

Sarah's body became racked with her sobs, and Nick pressed his foot down on the accelerator, his shoulders rigid with tension. The sooner they imparted this revelation to the police, the better. Nick secretly wondered if Sarah's hunch about the killer was a little far-fetched, but then he'd never worked with affection-starved young people and had zero idea of their capabilities.

CHAPTER 26

Dylan chewed the end of his pen nervously after Nick and Sarah left his office. The further statement provided by Sarah certainly fitted in with the updated information provided by Sandra Jones. It looked like they had their man. The problem was, they needed to tread carefully to ensure Shaun Wallace didn't do a runner before they arrested him on suspicion of the murders. Shaun was still currently nowhere to be found, much to the team's annoyance. Dylan was aware that the youth of today knew how to go underground, judging by the number of Missing Persons Reports that remained unsolved when kids ran away from home. Now that Shaun Wallace was living independently, he could go missing whenever he pleased. He'd certainly learned to stay hidden from the police's radar so far. *We need to move quickly on this, now that we have a ton of new information and further clues pointing to Shaun. It's now a case of obtaining DNA from him to prove he is the killer.*

Dylan sent Senior Constable Ben Norris over to Woodies to speak with Jock, who was clocking on for the afternoon shift. The police had requested copies of the most recent photo kept on file for Shaun, along with any valid file notes police were permitted to receive under the information-sharing guidelines. Dylan intended to take any new information to the briefing that afternoon and run everything past Gardner for further advice.

Norris was about to leave Woodies having gathered the required information, when Jock called him back into the office. 'Hang on, something has just occurred to me!' Norris stood patiently while Jock retrieved Shaun's file from the archives. Jock logged into the government data base to search Shaun's care history. 'Holy shit!'

Jock stared closer at the screen. He crooked his finger for the police officer to come over to take a closer look. Norris stared at the screen which displayed Shaun's care history. He'd been taken into care at seven years of age, placed with an aunt briefly and then resided at Woodies until he'd reached adulthood, having been unsuccessful at being matched with any potential foster carers. Any possible matches always ended up pulling out when they learned of his extreme behaviours and mental health issues. Norris looked at Jock pointedly and shrugged. *So what?*

Jock tapped the right-hand corner of the screen with his pen. Under the banner of respite care, the name Kate Jones was listed as a respite carer for Shaun. Given that it was a fairly common name, neither Sarah nor Jock had paid much attention to the Enfield murder story when it had aired, both being too caught up in what was going on for them at the time. The staff at Woodies certainly hadn't made any connection between the murder of this woman and the murders of Sarah's father and sister. But it suddenly seemed glaringly obvious that Sarah's hunch was right: Shaun seemed intent on targeting the women who'd featured prominently as mother figures in his life.

Norris's eyes rounded as the penny dropped that Jock had just provided another significant lead in the unsolved case. Due to confidentiality, the officer was unable to divulge to Jock that this added further weight to the statement recently provided by Sandra Jones, but Jock could tell from his expression that he'd given him crucial information that the police required to solve the case. Jock stared after the departing officer as the enormity of the situation suddenly sunk in. *Jings we never really know how these young people are going to turn out, do we?*

A few minutes later, Dylan's phone vibrated in his suit jacket pocket. He opened a text message from Norris who'd attached a clear photo of Shaun Wallace. The image was a little dated, having been taken when he turned eighteen just prior to his departure from care. A text message followed:

> This is a photo of Shaun Wallace just before he left care – so it was before he sported the jet-black hair and piercings. Jock the youth worker at Woodlands Residential Care Unit just confirmed Shaun's respite carer was called Kate Jones. Just thought I'd impart this info to you ASAP.

Dylan sat up straight in his chair. His pulse quickened as he read the text message confirming Shaun Wallace's connection to both murders. He stood up and stared blindly out of the window. Back in his day, he would have rung his boss to impart this information. There were no smart phones to send images and texts in the old days, however, so maybe it was unfair to compare. These young officers seemed to text faster than they could talk nowadays. This irritated Dylan slightly as he was old school in his communication methods. He smiled as he thought of what his nephew often said to him: *Move with the times, uncle, or move on!* He gave a soft chuckle. *I digress! The main thing here is that it's all coming together! But if he is The Riddler, how come he left no poem at the scene of the Port Elliot murders?*

Gardner stuck his head in at the doorway. 'Any news to report prior to the next briefing?'

Dylan nodded. 'Yes, boss. We have another strong lead on the current suspect for the murders of Paul and Jessica Henderson, and Kate Jones. I will explain in full to the team once Ben Norris returns to base. In the meantime, I have this photo of the suspect, sir. It fits with our other findings to date that all lead us back to the same person of interest.'

Dylan held up his phone displaying the image of Shaun Wallace. Gardner's stomach churned horribly as he pushed away another unwelcome flashback. His face remained impassive.

'See that you bring as much information to the table as you possibly can. You will need more than just an image of some gothic kid.' Gardner's tone was abrupt. He turned on his heel and walked off before Dylan could reply.

Dylan stared after his retreating superior with a sour expression. *What the hell is that cockhead's problem? Didn't I just say I will update him in due course? Of course we have more than just an image! Gardner is impossible to please!*

Gardner stormed into his office and slammed the door. The team knew better than to ask if he was alright as this was a sure sign he did not want to be disturbed. Gardner sat with his head in his hands, the all-too-familiar unwelcome trickle of sweat sliding down his back.

Gardner felt the angel on one shoulder and the devil on the other. His conscience seemed to constantly seesaw to the point where he was questioning his own sanity. Ever since Angela had announced she wanted a divorce, his moral compass was becoming increasingly questionable. Before, he'd have worried about his actions letting his wife and daughter down, but now that he had no one to let down, it was all too easy for everything to spiral out of control. *Shit, I'm sounding just like those errant kids that end up entering a life of crime because their parents don't care about them. Am I making excuses for my own behaviour?*

The constant battle to manage his addiction was an added layer of complexity. To his knowledge, none of his colleagues other than Dylan Mathews knew about it. Gardner believed Dylan would be cautious about spreading gossip regarding what he knew, but all the same, the fact that he *did* know only served to increase his intense dislike for the man. *Mathews is a great detective – highly skilled and efficient – possibly more skilled than me… wait! Why the hell am I letting myself think that? I'm losing my mind!*

Gardner rubbed his temples. He was becoming unhinged. Why was he doubting himself? Why did Dylan make him feel inadequate? Was he really threatened by the man's capabilities? Why did he allow those thoughts to creep in? *Dylan has dirt on you and the prick can use it as ammunition if he wants to, that's why.*

Everything was unravelling around him. Not only did Dylan know things he shouldn't, he now possessed a photo of a suspect that was unwelcome to Gardner. The image was of the very man whom Gardner was praying he would not have to see or deal with again.

The photo of the six-foot lanky boy was messing with his mind and creeping into his every thought. *I can't seem to concentrate on anything else.* The photo had been taken a couple of years ago. The boy had clearly dyed his hair and had had facial piercings done since then, but he was still recognisable as the same person. Gardner had suspected this man was the killer from the start and now he was shitting bricks. This was the boy that he'd failed to report to his superiors, despite his own hunches at the time. This was the boy he'd seen with blood on his boots around the time of the murders at Port Elliot. Instead of reporting it, he'd run as fast as he could. Because if the force found out he'd been frequenting the home of a known drug addict and prostitute, his career would be finished, just like his marriage was.

But I will keep going back for more because you can't rehabilitate a sex addict, right? No amount of therapy can fix it and it's costing me everything. What do I do? What do I do? What do I do?

Gardner made a snap decision. He would take a patrol car to go and visit the suspect off the record and based on how that exchange went, he would know what his next move should be. There was still a window of time before the next briefing.

As Gardner headed towards the grey-looking housing trust units where Shaun Wallace resided, he thought about his wife and daughter. Were they ever going to come around and forgive him? He'd worked his ass off all these years to provide for them and give them the holidays of a lifetime. They'd wanted for nothing. Yet in the blink of an eye, they'd turned on him, made him feel like he no longer existed. *I'm a sex addict, a vulgar pig; there is no turning back. If this Shaun Wallace kid can identify me as one of Loretta's clients, then I'm finished. He gave me a prolonged stare that night; he was definitely taking notes. Or is that my paranoia? Of course, I can deny ever having seen him; it's his word against mine. But in my haste to leave Loretta's, I left my sunglasses behind. Loretta said the guy who arrived after me took them… so, I'm screwed if he recognises me. My prints would be all over the sunglasses too…*

Gardner's head began to spin. As well as his concerns about the suspect identifying him as one of Loretta's customers, he was also still cringing at the memory of Angela telling him she'd confided in Marie Mathews. *Why Dylan's wife, of all people?* Angela had only gone and told Marie the whole sordid story of how their marriage was a sham because of his sex addiction. Gardner was still as furious about it now as he had been when he'd found out. He knew Marie was prone to gossip and would have told Dylan the unsavoury details for sure. He'd taken it out on Dylan ever since. Gardner wiped the sweat from his forehead with the back of his hand as he tried to calm his rapid breathing.

Who else knows? Am I already a laughing stock? I've seen the smug look on Matthews's face whenever our eyes meet. He knows alright. He is just biding his time to use it against me.

CHAPTER 27

Sarah checked in with Detective Sergeant Dylan Mathews about how the case was going. The detective reassured her that they were on track and intended to swoop at any moment on the ex-Woodies resident she was now so sure was the killer. Sarah felt determined not to let fear take over in order to go about her daily life as much as possible. She felt sure that Shaun Wallace must be under police surveillance by now and this gave her a false sense of bravado. Dylan had failed to mention to Sarah that they were yet to locate him.

Sarah's mum had become a recluse since the murders, and she was determined not to follow suit. Her heart twisted as she thought of her mum living alone in the family home. All Jean seemed to want to do was leaf through old family photo albums. Her mum's usual spotless house was now covered in dust and she barely remembered to eat. Jean consistently refused Nick and Sarah's offers for her to go and live with them for a while. Jean got mad when Sarah tried to clean or cook for her or suggest various services that could step in and help. After having her head snapped off several times, Sarah finally stopped asking.

Sarah went to see Jean as much as possible, trying to get her out of the house and to see a therapist, but in the end she'd sourced a counsellor who agreed to do home visits. Sarah decided it was the one thing she'd put her foot down about. Jean needed help and her daughter was determined not to give up until she received it. Sarah felt pained to see her usually vibrant and chirpy mum in such a state.

She'd lost the love of her life and a daughter, and sadly she'd never be quite the same again.

Sarah felt the loss of her father and sister deeply too, but she needed to remain strong and focus on her own family. She could not afford to go to pieces. For a while it felt like she and Nick were drifting apart, and it terrified her. They both seemed to be constantly staring into space, wrapped up in their own thoughts and playing the continuous blame game about how they could have done things differently to avoid what had happened. In the end they'd talked it out and realised it was ridiculous to blame either themselves or each other for the heinous crimes committed by the psychopath who had robbed them of two beloved family members.

Sarah decided she needed to feel human again. The time had come to get out of the house and do something she enjoyed. Otherwise she wasn't living; she was merely existing. She was no good to anyone like that. *I can't pour from an empty cup.* She needed to be a good mum to poor Finn, who was having his own struggles with grief and loss. Trying to explain to a small child that they would never see their grandfather or auntie again was beyond awful. Feeling determined, Sarah decided she would keep her word and go to the gym with her friend Stacey, as promised. Stacey had been on her back about it for ages and Sarah reluctantly agreed that she'd be no better than her mum if she didn't start doing things that brought her joy again.

That evening, Sarah glanced at Stacey with a relieved expression as the gym instructor finally started winding down the body attack class by switching tempo to a ballad for the cool down track. Sarah's cheeks were bright pink and her gym clothes were saturated with sweat. But for the first time since the murders she felt alive. The endorphin rush following the aerobic exercise class was just what she needed.

Darkness had fallen over the car park by the time the two women hugged and parted ways. Stacey set off first and waved at her friend as she exited the car park. Sarah felt a stirring of unease but wasn't sure why. *My intuition is usually right.* She thought she could smell petrol fumes when she'd approached the door on the driver's side and hoped petrol wasn't leaking from her car somehow.

As she turned on the headlights and cruised down Shepherds Hill road, the engine started to sputter, and her car began to shudder and jerk. Sarah glanced down and noted the light on the dashboard indicated the fuel tank was empty. Sarah frowned; her hunch must have been correct about having a petrol leak. But her car had only just been serviced and had had a full tank of petrol when she'd collected it, so it was quite odd. Sarah decided to pull off into a quiet side street to investigate, feeling uneasy about how dark it was in these parts. The street lighting was poor, to say the least, and was only adding to her unease. Sarah was just wondering if she should chance trying to make it to the nearest petrol station when she saw a police car coming towards her. *Great! I was about to call Nick and be the damsel in distress but now the local coppers can help me instead!*

Sarah flagged the police car down, hoping the driver would be a nice friendly cop, preferably female. She was impressed to note that the driver slowed right down as though they were already stopping to check out why she was hovering in the street looking worried. *It's obviously a quiet night and the cops are bored, hoping for something exciting to do, to pass the time. Maybe they can take me to the nearest service station so I can fill up my jerry can.* Sarah smiled sheepishly knowing how pathetic she'd sound when she gave them her sob story.

As the male driver of the patrol car got out and marched aggressively towards her, Sarah's eyes grew wide with fear. Something didn't feel right. She peered as her eyes adjusted to the dim light. As he came closer, her brain registered who he was. The hairs on the back of her neck bristled and as if in slow motion, she turned back towards her car in a scramble to get into the driver's seat in a bid to lock the door behind her. The perpetrator had a furtive glance around then whacked Sarah on the back of the head with the butt of his gun. As she slithered to the ground, he picked her up and dropped her into the open boot of the stolen police car. He thought about binding her wrists and ankles but when she came around, it could be fun to let her try and fight him. She'd never win.

The driver felt his hammering heart with one hand while he steered the patrol car with the other. Keeping the heartbreaker captive was the best idea he'd come up with in a very long time. He would still have to kill her, of course, but this way he could get some well-deserved answers from her first. He might even succumb to the idea of using a few old-fashioned torture techniques. He'd learned from killing Kate that it left a horrible emptiness when you no longer had the opportunity to get the explanation you so badly needed from the victim about their actions. He regretted the way he'd gone about that now.

But for now, his confidence was soaring! What a massive achievement! Not only had he done away with the dumb cop who'd come sniffing around but he'd even managed to take his car and kidnap Sarah. Butch couldn't stop laughing, he was on such a trip. He'd been laying low for a bit, but once again, he was primed for vengeance.

CHAPTER 28

Dylan sighed loudly with an air of despair. Gardner had not returned to base for the briefing or to clock off for his shift. In addition, the patrol car he'd taken had not been returned to the compound. His boss's mobile phone was going straight to voicemail. It was strange that he'd taken a marked patrol car when he normally used his own unmarked vehicle. The more Dylan thought about it, the more he considered that Gardner's behaviour had been increasingly odd lately. Dylan really wanted to go home but there was an obvious duty of care to check the whereabouts of his boss, given that his current location was unaccounted for. But no one liked to question senior staff about their movements either. *Especially ones who dislike you intensely and make your life hell at the best of times.*

Due to the crisis response aspect of the role, the police often found their day shifts ran into the afternoon shifts. At times the afternoon shift even ran into the night shift. The situation could not be helped but this rarely appeased the families of police officers who had other plans for them. Dylan rolled his eyes every time he had to ring his long-suffering wife to break the news to her that their plans would have to change yet again. Marie never accepted this was the nature of his job and constantly took it out on him as though it were his choice not to come home. Dylan's thoughts were broken as Belinda marched towards him, talking at a rapid rate as she approached.

'Boss, we have just received a frantic call from Nick Whitaker. Sarah was due back from a gym class over an hour and a half ago and is not answering calls to her mobile phone. She is normally super reliable and never deviates from her routines without checking in with her husband. From what we know, she learned to be vigilant after working in residential care with some of our finest young offenders. Given the recent murders of her father and sister, it's vital that we look into her disappearance immediately. Obviously, it's far too soon to lodge a missing person's report, but given her recent revelations about Shaun Wallace fitting the modus operandi of The Riddler, I reckon we get a search happening and a patrol over to his place to check straightaway, agreed?'

Dylan leapt up, snatching his jacket from the back of his chair as he spoke. 'Shit, that's not good. Can you and Norris head to the known address of Shaun Wallace straightaway while I contact her husband? Let's hope Wallace has come out of hiding. Get a patrol to cover Sarah's last known movements and get a triangulation set up on her mobile phone – let's go! Call in the job now and request backup; I won't be far behind.'

Dylan had a strong hunch they were about to encounter the crook that police nicknamed 'The Riddler'. This asshole obviously likened himself to the *Batman* character by leaving his riddles as clues for authorities to solve. *How lame.*

Dylan made the obligatory call to Marie while he was on the move to let her know he'd be late home from work.

Marie answered after the second ring in her usual snappy tone. 'Let me guess; you won't be home until late?' she spoke before he did.

Dylan raised an eyebrow. 'Yeah, you got it in one, darl.' *I can be abrupt too you know!*

Marie rolled her eyes; it was all so predictable. 'Okay, see you when I see you.'

Dylan's disgruntled wife ended the call before he could explain any further. At the other end, Dylan stared at his mobile phone for a few seconds before refocusing on the job at hand. *God, the wife is becoming a right old witch. I will be having words with her later.* But he knew he wouldn't have the energy to ask what was bugging her. He never did. That was half the problem; they didn't talk much anymore.

Marie slammed the fridge door in frustration. She'd made Dylan's favourite pasta dish that evening as she'd experienced a few pangs of guilt about how short she was being with him lately. But since the asshole would probably fall into bed long after her, he could have beans on toast for all she cared. The cold pasta was now in a container in the fridge. If he wasn't going to eat with her then she wasn't going to make any effort for him. Years ago, it hadn't bothered her that his job entailed long hours, but it was annoying the shit out of her lately. She knew it was irrational to blame him for something that was out of his control, but he could always change jobs if it bothered him as much as it bothered her.

It's because the kids have grown up and I don't know what to do with myself half the time. Maybe I also sometimes wonder if he is really working late? I never used to be insecure. Menopause is messing with my mind!

Escapism was the only answer. Marie changed into her bathers and climbed into the spa with a glass of white wine. Now that she was no longer cooking up a storm, she'd get a bit of hot action from her racy novel instead. She glanced down at her menopausal bloated belly and sighed. After rereading the same three lines of her novel, she put the book down and sipped her wine thoughtfully. It was time to face the truth. Both she and Dylan were guilty of letting themselves go and becoming less attentive towards each other as they'd reached middle age. Her husband irritated the shit out of her sometimes and she wasn't finding him as attractive as she once had. But Marie realised that he probably felt the same way, given how avoidant he was being lately. They were ignoring each other for increasingly long periods of time. But the truth was that she really missed him when he wasn't there. She couldn't win.

Marie was good friends with Gardner's soon-to-be ex-wife, Angela. She knew that the friendship caused issues now that they were separating. But why should it suddenly be inappropriate for the women to remain friends after all those years of being forced to act like obedient little police wives who made idle chit-chat at police work functions? When it had suited Dylan and Gardner, it was all fine and dandy. But Gardner became shitty about the friendship when things turned sour with Angela and he constantly took it out on Dylan at work now.

Marie realised that this caused ongoing issues for Dylan with his boss, but she would not be told who she could and couldn't be friends with. Marie knew damn well why Gardner had an issue with the friendship continuing post-divorce. It was because he was afraid of what Angela might divulge about their marital problems when the two women caught up. Gardner probably assumed that Marie would tell Dylan everything and he'd be right.

Dylan's boss was even more of a creep than she'd first thought. It turned Marie's stomach now to think of how often she'd socialised with him in the past. What the hell was wrong with him that he needed to indulge in so much sex? His addiction had destroyed his marriage. According to Angela, Gardner expected sex several times a day and went looking for it elsewhere when she'd finally had enough of his unwanted advances.

The final straw was when she'd found out that he'd been frequenting a brothel. Angela experienced a breakdown at the time and had gone to stay at her sister's house for a couple of weeks. Marie was sworn to secrecy about the reasons for the split, but she'd become paranoid that maybe Dylan was going to brothels too. It would explain the late nights and the fact that he rarely initiated sex with her anymore. Her imagination had gone into overdrive, so one night she'd stayed up waiting for him to ask him outright.

When Dylan came home that night and saw the empty wine bottle and Marie's crazed eyes, he knew there was little chance of enjoying a whisky while watching the football highlights, as he'd anticipated.

'Are you a dirty pervert just like Gardner?' Marie looked furious and Dylan was completely bewildered.

'Huh?' Dylan frowned in confusion. 'What the hell is going on, Marie? Have you lost the bloody plot?'

Marie squared up to Dylan, the alcohol fumes on her breath making him wince. 'I know all about Gardner going to brothels! Angela told me everything! Dirty bastard! Are you in on it too?'

Dylan thought his wife had lost her mind. 'What in god's name are you talking about?'

Marie looked at the genuine confusion on Dylan's face and suddenly felt hopeful that he really was in the dark about the reason for Gardner and Angela's separation.

Marie explained the whole sordid situation to Dylan who was suitably stunned. 'Shit, that's messed up! But what if Angela is making it up? We can't just take her word for it! Gardner cannot know that I've been made aware she is accusing him of this, or my life won't be worth living! As for me, do you really think I'd have the energy or the inclination to go to a brothel? For Christ's sake! What do you take me for?'

Marie's eyes suddenly filled with tears. 'Well, we don't really do it anymore, do we?'

Dylan's face softened as he hugged his wife. 'It's normal for things to die down a bit in that department as you get older. Also, I work crazy long hours. Shall we make a bit more effort to get back on track?'

Marie gave a small nod. 'Let me go and put your favourite lingerie on and we can see about working on it right now…'

Dylan gave a weak smile; he was utterly exhausted and really not in the mood but didn't want to hurt his wife's feelings. By the time Marie came back to the lounge in the lingerie that was now far too tight, Dylan was lying on the sofa snoring softly.

'Prick!' yelled Marie, as she stormed off to bed. She cried herself to sleep – yet another thing that the old her would never have done. Menopause was making her feel a little unhinged. Despite him agreeing to work on things, it appeared to Marie that Dylan would simply never find the time.

CHAPTER 29

Butch knew he didn't have a lot of time. Soon it would become evident that Sarah and the dumb prick cop were both missing. Given that he'd stolen the cop's car, he would need to hide it very soon. *How can it be this easy to gain possession of a cop car and kidnap the heartbreaker, all in one night? I could not make this shit up!*

As he drove towards the unused car port which was part of the unit block he lived in, he was glad it had a roller door attached. Most of them didn't because hardly anyone in the area could afford cars to put in them. Apparently, a previous tenant was sick of being the only one in the street with a car and had the roller door fitted on the car port to stop his car being vandalised. Thank god he had, because there was nowhere else to hide the cop car. At least it was under the cover of darkness; hopefully all the stoners who lived in the unit block would be none the wiser when he drove in and shut the roller door behind him. Butch gave a low chuckle; he was still tickled about the irony of Sarah helping him obtain his driver's licence. *If it wasn't for her, she wouldn't be in the boot of this cop car. What a hoot!*

Only a few hours earlier, Gardner had knocked on his door to question him about his whereabouts on the nights of the Port Elliot and Enfield murders. Butch had felt both horrified and excited at the same time.

They'd eyeballed each other warily in the doorway of Butch's unit. Butch thought he knew the shifty-looking cop from somewhere but couldn't think where, initially. He didn't feel that Gardner exuded much of a presence about him for a Senior Sergeant. If anything, he seemed a bit on edge, with his sweaty upper lip and bulging eyes.

Gardner had cautiously entered the unit, his eyes sweeping the lounge room as he walked behind the occupant. He thought he'd noted a hint of recognition in the kid's eyes, but he couldn't be sure. Gardner needed to tread carefully and consider the best way to play this because he was fairly sure this boy was indeed responsible for the unsolved murders. He glanced down at the suspect's feet. They were wide and large, and he looked a lot like the suggested identikit drawings. Gardner experienced a stab of fear. *Am I really standing in the home of The Riddler with no backup and with no one aware of my movements?* Gardner considered that this was not one of his smartest moves. The enormity of his own stupidity dawned on him. *I'm losing it. I'm making poor decisions based on fear. Shit, I just want to know if he recognises me or not!*

'Take a seat.' Butch pointed to a filthy grey fabric sofa covered in stains and cigarette burns. Gardner declined. He shouldn't have come; the kid had the eyes of a demon. Gardner managed to convince himself that the kid didn't have a clue who he was. Therefore everything was fine; he was good to go. He'd send a couple of officers back to bring him in and lock him up. There was no logic in taking the kid on by himself; it simply wasn't a smart move. The gothic-looking boy emanated a sinister vibe. There was something unnerving about him that he couldn't quite put his finger on. In a bid to create a quick exit, Gardner reached into the inside pocket of his jacket to locate his mobile phone. His intention was to feign that an urgent text message required him to leave promptly. But Butch assumed he was reaching for a weapon and impulsively smashed him hard on the top of his head with the brick he kept on his sideboard. His hunch that it would come in handy one day had been right.

Butch watched Gardner fall clumsily to the floor with a look of shock on his face as his head banged against the open door on the way down. The pig had clearly lost consciousness. Butch stood over him, watching the blood trickling down his face. He was fascinated at his own lack of remorse. The more he inflicted pain on others, the calmer he felt about it. Maybe being stoned helped; who knew? But what he'd just done to the cop meant he would definitely be going to prison and despite craving top-dog status, he was still conflicted over whether he was ready for that. Ultimately, this depended which personality he presented with on any given day.

Butch was about to check for a pulse out of curiosity rather than out of any care factor, when his eyes narrowed as he stared down at the podgy cop. He studied his victim's face, racking his brains. Suddenly it dawned on Butch who the dude was. *Got it!* This was the guy who'd fled from Loretta's on the night of the Port Elliot murders. Butch had seen him pounding into Loretta as though his life had depended on it, his fat ass on display for all to see. The podgy middle-aged man had taken off like a bat out of hell when Butch had turned up. *So he is a cop, hey? What a creep!* This would explain how he could afford Ralph Lauren sunglasses, though. Butch had pocketed them for himself when the moron left them behind at Loretta's.

If Butch hadn't been craving sex that night, he would have chased the fat bloke down the street that night, just for the thrill of it. But it was true that committing murder was an aphrodisiac; he'd been way too horny to think of anything else at that moment. Butch had always wondered if that was a myth, but now he could tick off *that* little mystery once and for all. Suddenly feeling possessive about Loretta, he picked up the bloodied brick and smashed Gardner's face to a pulp, then calmly made sure there were no longer any signs of life. Loretta shouldn't have to put up with having sex with men like this. *The filthy animal deserved it.*

As soon as it was dark outside, Butch grabbed Gardner under his arm pits and dragged his body next door, depositing it next to the skip in the driveway. The occupants generally existed in a hazy drug-induced state so were unlikely to make a fuss about it. He then emptied the contents of several of the tenants' wheelie bins over the top of him. It didn't look too out of place. The street was always littered with rubbish; it was that kind of neighbourhood. It was highly possible that he'd been seen by someone and it was highly probable that he was leaving way too many clues that would lead more cops straight to his door. Butch shrugged; he felt indifferent. *What will be will be.* First, he needed to deal with the pressing issue of what he planned to do about Sarah. There was still work to do before it all caught up with him. *The finale!* Butch doubled over with laughter. *I am definitely insane – whoop, whoop!*

CHAPTER 30

Sarah opened her eyes, the back of her head throbbed horribly. She experienced a fleeting flashback of her head hitting the pavement and shuddered. As her eyes adjusted to her surroundings, she realised she was somewhere unfamiliar. She was lying on a filthy mattress in a dingy room. The sheets reeked of body odour and stale urine. *Oh my god, I was attacked and abducted. This can't be real.*

She was startled by a monotonous male voice coming from the other side of the room. 'Hello Sarah, long time no see!'

Sarah tried to sit up but felt too dizzy and gingerly lay back down again. Her voice came out as a croak. 'Shaun, is that you? Why are you doing this?'

Butch stared blankly at the woman he'd looked up to for all those years. He'd thought she was a saint but now he could see her for what she really was. He stood over her with his arms folded as he spoke.

'I could have tied you up and tortured you, Sarah, and maybe I still will, but first I want some fucking answers!'

Sarah used all her willpower to sit up. It was a struggle, but this time she managed. *I need to stay calm and remember my training. I know a bit about how his mind works.*

Sarah cleared her throat, trying to buy more time to ensure whatever she said wouldn't inflame the situation. 'Shaun, is this about the way I left Woodies? Do you feel that I let you down? After reflecting I can totally understand how this would have impacted you and I regret not taking a more sensitive approach. But I was pregnant at the time and I…'

Butch belted Sarah hard across the face before she could finish her sentence. As she felt her lip swell and tasted the blood on her tongue, she realised with disdain that it was unlikely she'd find any words to appease him.

Butch's face was contorted; he bared his rotten teeth as he snarled at her. 'You fucking broke me, you bitch! You left me at Woodies to rot! You let me transition into independence without your help! You were my mentor for years! The one constant in my life! How could you just fucking walk away and leave me hanging like that?'

Butch punched Sarah in the face again and her head swung violently to one side as blood spurted from her nose.

'By the way, my name isn't Shaun anymore. He died along with your memory. You can call me Butch, you dumb bitch!'

Sarah's eyes began to puff and swell. She was in agony and felt sure her nose was broken. She sat there in miserable silence, knowing that whatever she said now was likely to inflame him further. Sarah felt dizzy – close to passing out – but she needed to keep her wits about her if she wanted to live. She desperately wanted to lie down again but knew it would be a fatal mistake.

Butch began to pace up and down. 'I want some fucking answers, so you better start talking. I've known you since I was seven years old. You and Jock were the only youth workers who looked past my background and treated me like a human being. How could you just disappear from my life and treat me like I'm a nobody?'

Sarah forced herself to concentrate on his words. Was she imagining that he was close to tears? He'd never been one to show emotion in all the years she'd known him. *Did I make the biggest mistake of my life walking away from those kids the way I did? Maybe I was selfish, self-centred and cowardly. Did I really think Shaun would get over my departure from his life? Deep down I knew there would be an impact but was it so wrong to walk away with no explanation to protect my unborn baby?*

Sarah bowed her head in anticipation of the next blow. She knew it would come, whether she spoke or not. She looked around the room through her half-shut swollen eyes, trying to figure out where the exits were. Sarah noted a window to her left and a door straight in front of her. She doubted he'd take his eyes off her long enough for her to attempt any form of escape.

Sarah's voice was a faint rasp. 'I should have known better. I let all of you down when I left Woodies. I should have been honest with you all. I should have explained why I was leaving and told you all in person when I decided not to return. I was afraid for my unborn child. I hope you can understand that. Just before I left, another female youth worker at another unit was attacked by the residents while pregnant. I was terrified of that happening to me at Woodies and I took the coward's way out. I guess I'm now paying the price. I am truly sorry, Shaun, I....'

Butch flew at her and struck her jaw once more. 'My name is not fucking Shaun' it's Butch! Get that into your thick skull!' He grabbed a fistful of Sarah's hair and pulled her head backwards. 'What's my name?'

Sarah's eyes met his soulless grey ones and a stream of fresh tears trickled down her face. 'Butch,' she whispered.

Shaun pulled her hair back further. 'Louder!' His sour breath was hot on her skin.

Sarah winced at the foul stench and mustered up as much energy as possible to make her voice louder. 'Butch.'

Her captor suddenly laughed as he let her hair go. 'That's my name; don't wear it out!'

Butch began pacing again. Sarah's left eye was beginning to close; her face felt puffy and alien. She was wondering how long she'd been missing for and whether her car and phone had been located. *I can't lose my wits here; I can't give up. Nick and Finn need me, and I will be damned if our family is going to suffer any more loss! Nick must've alerted the police by now. They have to be on their way here, please god.*

'Guess where we are going now?' Butch did not take his eyes from her as he reached into his bag for the stolen gun. Sarah's blood turned to ice. *Please god; it's not my time yet. Please, no.*

'We are going up to the roof, that's where! You think I don't know the cops will be on to me? This is my moment! My five minutes of fame! But this way, I control how long this fucking takes and I decide when to pop your head like a melon in front of everyone – pop, pop, pop!'

Sarah's stomach churned with fear as bile rose in her throat. Butch grabbed her from the bed and forced her to stand in front of him so he could point his gun into her back. She swayed as she tried to steady herself.

'You are looking pretty unbalanced there, Sarah! Maybe you will slip on the way up and it will be over quicker than you think!'

Butch howled with laughter. He'd already set up a stolen ladder at the side of the block of units. He propelled Sarah forward until she was standing in front of it. 'Up we go!' He gave an insane cackle right behind her.

Sarah felt the gun dig into her spine and knew she needed to find the strength to do as he asked. She climbed each rung slowly, hesitantly, her limbs shaking uncontrollably. *I can't pass out now; I must keep going. I need to get up there and find a way to get off the roof. His mental health is beyond repair. He is a danger to society, to the remaining members of my family.*

Fighting her vertigo, Sarah kept looking downwards, concentrating on her gym shoes as she scrambled up to the roof. Butch was right behind her. He produced her mobile phone from the pocket of his hooded jumper as he kept the gun trained on her with his other hand.

'I hope you have Jock's number in this phone cos you are gonna ring him and ask him to be my spokesperson! Then you can ring your husband and bratty kid to say goodbye!'

Butch's deranged laugh rang out into the open sky. A magpie screeched back at him as though in agreement with his words. He handed the phone to Sarah. 'Get Jock here right now! I want the cops to talk to me via him! I won't talk to anyone else, especially not the filthy pigs!'

Sarah tried to focus on slowly breathing oxygen into her lungs to prevent herself from having a panic attack. *In through my nose and out through my mouth. I must keep calm; I must not pass out.* She took her mobile phone from Butch. Her head felt like wool. It was hard to focus on the contacts list, but she knew there was no choice but to do as he'd asked. With shaking hands, she rang Jock's number, hating that she'd need to involve him in this horrific mess. As he lived in the hills, she questioned how close by he would be, if he were off duty. Not that she knew her exact location, but she'd a fair idea of where she was. Jock had mentioned the housing units that Beth had transitioned to, only recently. Sarah remembered it was where Jock said he'd spotted Shaun in the street. *Maybe this isn't even Shaun's place, though. Maybe I'm being held captive somewhere else altogether!*

There was the potential for this to go horribly wrong because time was not on their side. Relief flooded through Sarah when Jock answered after the second ring.

'Hello there, ma love!' Jock's cheerful voice seemed so out of place at the other end, given the grim situation she was in. Sarah stammered, trying to get the words out in a coherent manner.

'Jock, listen carefully. Sha… sorry, Butch… he has me up on a roof. He says you are the only one he will speak to about it and….'

Jock cottoned on immediately and correctly guessed Sarah was being held captive by Shaun Wallace. The name Butch threw him initially but he knew enough about split personalities to understand they often liked to be known as different names, depending on the persona they were presenting at any given time. It was one hell of a coincidence that he happened to be in the area as he'd just finished helping another young person build some flat-packed furniture, following her transition into independent living. Given that he'd seen Shaun in the area only recently, he knew he was still living in the same housing trust units as a couple of other ex-Woodies residents. Jock was only around the corner.

As if to confirm his thoughts, Butch called out his address in the background. 'Make it snappy, Jock, and no cops – just you!'

Jock's cheery tone changed to a serious one. 'I'm not too far away. Give me a couple of minutes.'

Butch ended the call, satisfied with Jock's response.

Without hesitation Jock sprang into action. He knew he needed to try his best to talk Shaun down from his position on the roof with poor Sarah. *I cannae believe he has taken Sarah captive! Whit the hell is going on! My pal is at imminent risk at the hands of a depressed, possibly suicidal, delusional and cold-blooded young man. Please let this end well.*

'Now ring your husband,' Butch spat.

Sarah speed-dialled Nick, who answered his phone after the second ring. 'Sarah! Where the hell are you? I've been out of my mind with worry.'

Sarah heard the anguish in his voice and her eyes filled with fresh tears. Her voice was so hoarse now that it hurt her throat to speak. She looked at Butch warily. He hadn't told her what to say; he was leaving it to her, which was increasing her unease.

'Nick,' she whispered, unsure of what to say.

Nick cut in immediately. 'Sarah! What's going on? I thought that psycho kid might have got his hands on you. I thought...'

Sarah cut in before he said anything further to inflame Butch.

'Nick, I'm not a hundred percent sure where I am, but I reckon your hunch could be right.' Sarah began to sob as Butch looked on with cold hard eyes. 'I love you and Finn so much. I'm so sorry.'

Butch snatched the phone and clicked it off as Sarah's knees buckled, her body racked with sobs. *Please don't let me die here. He has never been able to show mercy to anyone, not in the whole time I knew him. How could I not have seen this coming?*

'Get up!' Butch barked. Sarah attempted to straighten up her sinking body, willing herself to muster what little strength she had left.

Butch smirked. He knew that everything was closing in on him and he'd be unable to draw out the murder investigations any further. He'd enjoyed imagining the faces of the baffled cops when they read his riddles. Butch often fantasised about the police sniffing around asking the locals what they knew about him and his recent movements. The imagined scenario made him feel important. Another favourite daydream was where he imagined himself being non-compliant during police interviews. Butch likened himself to one of those smart killers on the television show *Wire in the Blood.* His dream was to be remembered as one of those killers who drive police mad with their calm demeanour and blunt answers to leading questions. *No comment!* But sadly, there was no time for any of that. The whole thing was all going to come to a head today instead. He was seriously considering ending his own life as well as Sarah's. *But, wait! I can't decide if I want to live or die. Maybe Shaun wants to live and Butch doesn't. I don't even know who I am today.*

Butch had hidden the boots and clothes he'd worn during his killing sprees knowing full well that the police needed those items to pin the murders on him. Little did Sarah know the evidence was right there, up on the roof, not far from where he was holding her at gunpoint. Her father and sister's blood spatters were on the evidence in the black bin liner close to where she was standing. Butch let out an unbalanced-sounding laugh, and Sarah shrank in terror. *I thought*

I knew how to manage him, but I was so wrong. You can't reason with a psychopath who has no conscience.

As Butch waited for Jock to arrive, he thought again about how badly he wanted the recognition for the murders so he could be the top dog in prison, once the charges were laid. But the flip side of his personality considered that prison would be terrifying and that he may in fact not be top shit there after all. Butch was split down the middle about his feelings regarding the whole thing. He wasn't dumb; he knew both Sarah's husband and Jock would have called the cops by now, even though he'd said not to. The police would have traced Sarah's mobile phone, regardless. *This is what I wanted, isn't it? For an audience to watch from down below while the authorities waste all their precious resources on me. Hell, yeah!*

Suddenly an involuntary nervous tick made his head twitch. Butch blinked angrily, feeling uncertain about his final goal. All he knew was that at this precise moment, he could taste vengeance. Butch felt no remorse for his victims and the impact of their deaths on their significant others; he only felt a ripple of apprehension about the impact it may have on him in the long term. It occurred to him that the best outcome would be to get all the accolades for the crime without having to do the time. *Well, whaddya know; it rhymes!* He chuckled as the idea came to him. He suddenly knew exactly what to do. Or did he? He likened his current thought process to a malfunctioning terminator. *Terminate the target. Don't terminate the target. I can change my mind like the wind!*

Butch scanned the roof and spotted the black bin liner containing the incriminating blood-spattered boots and clothes. He smirked as he considered it was a miracle they were still up there in one piece. The bag had not been secured in any way. Thankfully, the weather had been kind to them lately. He bent slightly to snatch it up with his free hand while keeping the gun firmly pointed in Sarah's back with the other.

CHAPTER 31

As promised, Jock promptly arrived at the address provided by Butch and headed towards the housing trust units with a determined march. Despite Butch telling him not to alert the police, he'd called Detective Sergeant Dylan Mathews on the way to tell him about the situation. Jock emphasised the importance of police referring to Shaun as Butch if they wanted to get on his good side and bargain with him. Dylan assured Jock that police were already on their way due to other information received and advised Jock under no circumstances to approach Butch, despite his demands.

But Jock knew that if anyone could reason with Butch, it would be him and not a police negotiator. He was willing to take the chance, as it was not an option to sit back and do nothing when Sarah knew he was the only other person Butch had a good rapport with. As he got closer, he yelled up to Butch.

'Right, I'm coming up that ladder to talk to you. Is that okay?'

Butch yelled back down to him. 'Come on up! It's time to join the party, Jock!'

As Jock approached the top rung of the ladder, he focused on the best way to connect with Shaun, or Butch, as he now wanted to be known as. Finding a mutual interest was how he usually engaged with young people and it hadn't failed so far. Jock remembered Shaun was interested in Scottish football and they'd often joked about how it was called soccer in Australia. Whenever Jock was on duty at Woodies unit, they'd chat about Jock's favourite team, the Glasgow Rangers.

Given that Shaun had looked up to Jock as a male role model, he had soon become a fan of the same football team and they'd formed a bond. Every time Jock worked with Shaun, they would discuss how Rangers were performing and it gave them something in common.

Maybe I can get him into a headspace where we chat aboot stuff just like the old days? I need tae think carefully here! Not only is what I say important, but I've got tae be careful about what not to say. Jings! I'm up for the challenge if it means saving Sarah.

Jock approached the scene cautiously. He remembered the Behavioural Change Stairway Model training he'd undertaken as part of his youth worker induction. The youth workers needed a certain skill set in case the residents ended up taking each other hostage. Young people in care were known to do such crazy things. *What were the four steps again? First I huv tae start with active listening, then show empathy, then build rapport, and then use my influence to hopefully lead to a change in behaviour.*

As Jock edged closer, the look of triumph on Shaun's face was not lost on him. *Shit, I need tae remember tae call him Butch instead of Shaun or I will lose here!*

'Hey Butch, what's this all aboot then?'

Jock played it cool while noting that Sarah was in bad shape. She looked completely out of it, like she was on another planet and ready to pass out. Butch's eyes swept over Jock, his expression impassive, but he was secretly pleased that his old youth worker had come to speak with him. Not only that, but he'd addressed him as Butch, which was a sign of respect as far as he was concerned. Jock had always been good at that. The youth worker focused on what mattered to the kids at Woodies.

But Sarah was the one he'd become obsessed with. Butch glanced down at his hostage as he spoke with Jock. 'She fucked me over, Jock. Left me behind like a bag of trash! She walked away from Woodies without a backward glance and gave zero fucks about me!'

Sarah was listening intently to every word but was too frozen with fear to dare comment. She felt tender and bruised from the constant pressure of the gun barrel digging into her back. Sarah knew Jock could sense her terror and felt comforted to feel the calm presence of her old workmate. Jock caught her eye briefly and tried to give her his best reassuring look before he addressed her captor.

'I'm listening tae ye, Butch. Believe me, I want tae understand your side o' things. You sound pretty upset aboot the way Sarah left the unit, and I totally get that. I know Sarah well, just like you do. I can promise you wholeheartedly that she did care aboot ye and still does. It was a difficult situation for her when she left. I know fae talking wi her that she wonders if she could have tackled her departure in a different way. I'm not discounting or minimising how ye feel, Butch, not one bit. I'm just letting ye know that the way she departed doesn't suddenly mean that all yer years in her care at Woodies count for nothing.' Jock deliberately paused to allow his words to sink in. Butch's expression remained blank.

Jock glanced down at the sea of anxious faces that had suddenly appeared in the street below. Jock looked back at Butch who was scowling.

'I thought I said no cops!'

Jock gave his best exasperated expression and shrugged. 'I didn't call them, mate. But, if ye are gonnae climb on a roof wi a hostage then there is a gid chance yer neighbours will call the cops, doncha think?'

Butch found Jock's comment highly amusing and let out a mad-sounding laugh. He'd forgotten what a hoot Jock was. If he was honest, he was completely digging the whole scene below. The cops were cordoning off the area and no doubt going to attempt to talk him down at any minute.

Feeling relieved that he'd maintained Butch's trust, Jock rushed out his words. 'I think we can work together tae solve this problem that we have got here. We always got oan well, didn't we?'

Butch nodded reluctantly. He'd missed hearing Jock's Scottish accent on a regular basis. There was something mildly comforting about it.

'You are an intelligent laddie, Butch. What are yer intentions here and what is it ye hope to achieve?' Jock inwardly shuddered as his eyes met Butch's flat grey ones.

Jock suddenly jerked backwards as Butch unexpectedly yelled out. 'I killed Kate, my old respite carer!'

Jock felt sick to his stomach, but his expression did not change. *Think carefully before you answer. Don't show judgement; stay calm.* Jock noted Butch's Adam's apple bobbing furiously up and down in his throat. A sure sign he was agitated. Except they were not at the residential care unit now. The situation couldn't be contained like a regular critical incident.

Jock spoke softly. 'Did killing Kate give you the outcome you hoped for afterwards, Butch?'

Butch stared at Jock for a few seconds, then slowly shook his head. Jock was stunned when Butch spoke honestly about it.

'It made me feel empty inside, Jock. It didn't feel that good afterwards, to be honest.'

Jock glanced at Sarah. She was becoming floppy and beginning to whimper incoherently. Jock kept his cool and prayed his next question was the right one.

'I bet there were lots of questions you wished you had asked Kate but never got the chance, right? Maybe answers that you need for closure so you could move on fae the past?'

Butch silently nodded in agreement. Feeling encouraged, Jock continued. 'So how aboot you don't do the same thing to Sarah, then? We could all get doon fae here and when Sarah is up to it, she could talk to you about how you felt when she left Woodies? That way, you are in control and hold the power. You get to ask her all the things you don't understand about this whole thing?'

Butch considered this option, his head cocked to one side. He was suddenly feeling exhausted and couldn't remember the last time he'd eaten. His drug rush was wearing off too. Maybe Jock made a good point. He'd already killed a few people so would be going to prison anyway. He'd be getting all the adulation he needed when he was top dog. He really could do with getting some coherent answers from Sarah. She obviously wasn't up to it at the moment, though. But, should he even give her that chance when she clearly didn't deserve it? *Or I could just blow all three of us away here and now! Pop, pop, pop! Am I Butch or am I Shaun? No, I'm The Riddler! Do I want to live, or do I want to die? I can change my mind like the wind!*

Jock could see the inner turmoil play out on Butch's face and knew he was running out of time to contain the situation. The cops would have to take over and they may have to shoot him, if it came to that. It was not going to end well, no matter what.

Jock gave it one last try. 'Shall the three of us get off this roof and get cheeseburgers from McDonald's, just like old times? We could talk about how well Rangers are playing at the moment?

To Jock's astonishment, Butch looked keen. 'Yeah, let's do that. Tell the cops I've agreed we can all come down and I will talk.'

Jock gestured down to Detective Sergeant Dylan Mathews, who was getting a sore neck from his eyes being glued upwards towards the scene on the roof. Jock gave him a triumphant thumbs-up sign. Jock could tell the detective was mighty pissed off that he'd not followed the advice to wait for police to arrive and decide how to manage the situation. *Oh, well! I know it's unlikely that the police would get anywhere talking tae the laddie. I had tae do ma bit.*

Jock was well aware that Butch's split personality meant that he needed to strike while the iron was hot. The kid could change his mind in the blink of an eye.

Jock spoke rapidly. 'Can you trust me to let the cops help Sarah get back down? She isn't going to manage on her own; she looks close to passing out.'

Butch nodded. He was suddenly feeling sleepy. He made Jock jump again as he unexpectedly blurted out, 'It was me! I did the Port Elliot murders! The evidence is right here in the black bag on this roof!'

Jock managed to continue hiding his true feelings but felt physically sick as he glanced at the black bin liner. God only knew what gruesome findings were in there. The kid was clearly psychotic, but now was not the place to get into it with him. Hopefully he would fully confess to the police waiting eagerly below. Jock had worked with enough kids who'd moved from juvenile justice to the adult prison system to know that they craved the recognition for their crimes. Often it was the only praise they received in life. This was the only thing they currently had on their side. Jock reckoned a part of Shaun really wanted to experience a pat on the back from his peers. Shaun might even be able to reconnect with certain ex-Woodies residents if he ended up in prison.

CHAPTER 32

Dylan felt apprehensive, the strain evident on his lined face. His head pounded, his eyes ached, and lack of sleep was making him a little highly strung. *We still haven't figured out where the hell Gardner is! Some negotiator! I don't think he'd approve of what we are doing here, but what choice do we have when Shaun Wallace refuses to speak with anyone but Jock?*

Dylan gave a defeated sigh. This Jock character was a brave man, but he'd put himself at risk going up to the roof. Even though he was likely to be the only one to talk sense into the kid, the police still had a duty of care to keep him safe. Jock had given the thumbs-up sign indicating that Shaun Wallace had agreed to come down from the roof. But now they appeared to be stalling. The young lad appeared to be too busy basking in his moment of glory to come down any time soon.

Dylan would deal with any backlash from Gardner afterwards, if he ever decided to show up! *Where the hell was he?* He inhaled sharply. *I can only deal with one thing at a time.* Dylan's primary concern was getting Sarah and Jock down safely and containing Shaun. Sarah's distraught husband was becoming distressed to the point where he was a hindrance and was currently being calmed down by another officer. Nick's parents were taking care of Finn and Sarah's mother was yet to find out about the situation. The family were trying to keep it from her, fearing it would tip her over the edge. Therefore, the recent media presence was creating further anxiety for the family. Nick prayed that his mother-in-law would not be following the current news headlines.

Ben Norris followed what was going on via his police radio as he sped towards the scene to join the mayhem of police, paramedics and the fire brigade. Everyone had different theories about the best way to engage with Shaun Wallace but all eyes were still on Jock.

Butch's eyes glittered as he looked down at them all. He felt euphoric. Why had he not thought of this sooner? *For once, all eyes are on me! Look how many resources are being wasted on little old me! What a hoot!*

Dylan's eyes were still trained on Jock talking with Shaun but he could sense the frustrated energy of the crowd. He could not prolong this any longer. Dylan raised his megaphone as he noted that Shaun was teetering dangerously close to the edge of the roof with Sarah in tow. Jock was talking animatedly with him, looking composed and in control. Dylan secretly admired the guy. Jock was either a natural in high-danger situations or he was a bloody good actor. Somehow he suspected it wasn't the latter. *He would make a bloody good cop.*

Dylan composed himself before using his best authoritative, yet friendly, voice.

'It's okay, mate. We can see that you have a lot going on for you right now and you are feeling a bit overwhelmed. How about you, Jock and Sarah come down so we can have a proper chat about it? It would be good to get you down here so we can hear your side of things. What do you reckon?'

Dylan could see the extent of Sarah's fear as he assessed her body language. She was slouched, her shoulders slumped forward in defeat; her head hung low. She was slipping away. *Shit, we need to take control sooner rather than later.*

Jock looked on, perplexed, his lips pursed in a frustrated line. He'd been so close to getting Butch to come down from the roof, he was sure of it. He kind of wished the police didn't have to intervene but understood there was no choice. Butch laughed at the collective morons below. What a trip! He was loving every moment of this. He dropped the bag to cup his hand around his mouth so he could yell down to them.

'Let me put you punks out of your misery and tell you what is in this bag!' Butch snatched up the black bin bag and waved it in the air triumphantly as though it were the queen's jewels.

A bystander standing behind the area cordoned off by police was filming the exchange on his mobile phone. This was not lost on Butch and he savoured it, a menacing smile crossing his lips. He wondered how many times the video would be viewed, and by whom. The recording would go viral! This was his only chance to get his performance down pat! There were no rehearsals for the big moment. No siree! A surge of adrenaline coursed through him as his Adam's apple bobbed up and down in his neck.

Butch tried to maintain direct eye contact with Dylan, his legs spread in a confident stance, his expression smug. He held the black bin bag aloft once more and dug the gun further into Sarah's back with his free hand. If he needed to, he could use the bag of evidence as a bargaining tool. Sarah winced in pain. Butch was becoming irritated with how floppy she was becoming. If she keeled over and fell off the roof of her own accord, then the fun would come to an end too soon. He lunged backwards with Sarah in tow, to ensure they wouldn't fall over the edge. Butch yelled down at the growing crowd, impressed that he'd memorised the rhyme he'd thought of only hours earlier.

'Riddle me this:
What's in this bag?
Maybe a pair of boots, a bloodied rag?

Riddle me this:
Why did they die?
Because they lied, looked me in the eye.

Riddle me this:
Why did they pretend to care?
Mess with my feelings – how could they dare?'

Dylan grimaced. This guy was The Riddler, without a doubt. This was the killer. But what were the chances of getting Sarah Whitaker down safely? *Where the hell is Gardner and the missing patrol car? I need to park that thought for now and focus on the job at hand. I sincerely hope he hasn't done something stupid; he hasn't been in a great headspace since his separation from Angela.*

Dylan's instinct told him that Shaun Wallace was not capable of showing mercy. If he was also experiencing suicidal ideation, as suspected, then they could be in trouble here. Beads of sweat formed on Dylan's brow. He checked in with the rest of the team. Neither Gardner nor the patrol car he'd taken had been located as yet and unease was growing amongst the officers. The GPS tracker on Gardner's car had been disabled and that was yet another mystery. They were still working on tracing his mobile phone.

Sarah's car had been located not far from the gym she'd attended shortly before her disappearance and her mobile phone had been tracked to Shaun Wallace's residence. He was playing them for sure, but what was his next move? Dylan was desperate for Shaun to come down in one piece so they could interview him and get to the bottom of it all.

Jock had seemed so close to bringing him down only minutes ago. It was unclear why Shaun was stalling now. Every second seemed like an hour and Dylan was concerned that the showdown with Shaun was going on for far too long. He realised that his lack of success in building a rapport with him was prolonging things. He'd even go as far as admitting that Jock would probably have succeeded in the task at hand by now, if he'd not interfered.

Butch narrowed his eyes. He could sense the frustration emanating from the various figures of authority down below. He realised he needed to give them something if he wanted to keep his moment of glory going.

He waved the gun in Dylan's direction. 'Okay, we are coming down, but I want a Big Mac with fries and coke first!'

Dylan almost laughed out loud. This was absurd. The kid had clearly been watching too many unrealistic cop dramas on television! Yet it was a simple request and despite hating the thought of dancing to his tune, it was worth a shot, to give him a sense of power and control. Dylan flapped a hand at Norris, indicating he was to follow through with the request.

'Okay Shaun, consider it done. Your McDonald's meal is on the way. But you have to stick to your side of the bargain, right?'

Butch was enraged that he'd been referred to as Shaun instead of Butch and lurched forward, making Sarah's feet skid backwards in a desperate bid not to go over the edge of the roof. Butch shoved her hard in the back with his gun as he roared down at the crowd. 'My name isn't fucking *Shaun* anymore, its *Butch*! Got it?'

'Shit, he is really starting to lose it. I don't think we have much time on our hands,' Dylan hissed to his colleagues.

He was kicking himself that he'd forgotten to call him Butch instead of Shaun, despite being aware of the importance of this. Now he'd messed up his chances of maintaining a rapport with the kid. It was a major rookie error. This whole debacle would be pulled apart by his seniors and he wasn't looking forward to it. Dylan glanced upwards. Sarah was in bad shape; they would need to act before Norris returned with the food. Dylan tried not to lose eye contact in a bid to maintain his trust.

'Okay Butch, I'm sorry. I forgot that you prefer to be known by that name. I will make sure the other police officers are aware and it won't happen again.'

Ben was in a trance as he drove to the nearest McDonald's. The situation seemed surreal and he couldn't believe he was off to buy a meal for the asshole who was more than likely guilty of the recent heinous murders. He stopped at a red light, willing it to change so he could complete his mission and get back to the action in a timely manner. Ben drummed his fingers impatiently on the steering wheel.

The kid is probably a product of his shitty family environment. It's pretty damn tragic. Resolving a hostage crisis requires the use of every type of skilled communication strategy in the crisis intervention skill box. Gardner is supposedly the best negotiator we have, so where the hell is he? I don't have a good feeling about him...

Dylan's throat was beyond parched. His skin felt clammy and his shirt was plastered to his back. He desperately needed Panadol and water but was aware that he was in the midst of the most dangerous period during the hostage crisis. The first thirty minutes were generally when confusion and panic set in. Dylan could see that Shaun was wavering between showing strong emotions and ambivalence. The combination could spell disaster if he was as unhinged as police suspected. In an ideal world, the police negotiator would be the one doing all the talking but since no one was getting anywhere and the kid clearly only wanted to speak directly with Jock, the police felt there was no choice but to take a chance on the youth worker. No one could afford to further inflame the situation. Dylan felt sure Jock was doing a good job. He seemed to have a great rapport with young people, from what he'd learned about him to date. *It's likely this will end in a tactical assault to rescue Sarah. If the negotiation fails and he threatens to take her life, then shooting the kid may be the only option. This is turning out to be the shift from hell.*

CHAPTER 33

Ben was deep in thought as he walked at a brisk pace, the brown paper McDonald's takeaway bag tucked under one arm. It was annoying that he had had to park slightly further away, given the number of vehicles now on the scene. Ben tutted at the inconvenience. The officer highly doubted Shaun Wallace was going to come down from the roof as promised, let alone allow Sarah to go free. The whole thing was absurd and far-fetched – surely the kid would not want his airtime to be over too soon. *Nah, no way; he is playing us, trying to maintain control. Why would he turn himself in? He knows he is going down for his crimes. The kid has other plans, no doubt.*

To Ben's astonishment when he glanced upwards as he approached Shaun's unit, he noted the trio were slowly being taken down from the roof safely by the police and fire brigade. Sarah was whisked straight to the back of the waiting ambulance where she promptly threw up into a sick bag; her eyes turning black due to her broken nose. Ben shook his head in wonderment; you really could not predict the way these situations would end. No one would have guessed in a million years that they all would have come down from the roof in one piece. *Whatever this Jock dude said to talk the perp into coming down worked!*

The other officers were stunned. It was truly a bizarre and unexpected outcome. Police seized Shaun's gun and he didn't resist. The surly young man sat in handcuffs in a contained area with police, his complexion grey and his expression blank. Shaun agreed to confess to the Port Elliot and Enfield murders and give a full statement, once he'd eaten his Big Mac.

Dylan uncuffed one of Shaun's hands, ensuring that his free hand was cuffed to the metal bar inside the police van. Norris handed Dylan a small bottle of water which he gratefully glugged down. Shaun bit into his burger, bits of food spraying everywhere as he spoke with his mouth full.

'By the way, if you are looking for that cop who came to question me earlier, you will find him dead under the pile of rubbish beside the skip next door to my place'.

Shaun pointed casually to his neighbour's driveway as the juices from the burger trickled down his hand.

'Oh, and his patrol car is right there in my car port; go and have a look.'

Dylan's heart almost stopped as his blood froze in his veins. As the detective's eyes met Shaun's he supressed a shiver as he experienced a new spike of fear.

Shaun had made these statements so casually, but Dylan felt it in his bones that the boy wasn't lying.

Dylan braced himself for the worst and formed a huddle with the other officers, where he quietly gave out instructions. If they were going to uncover a body, they could really do without the presence of the media and the crowd that continued to grow by the second. Given that the whole street was cordoned off, it only piqued the neighbours' interest all the more.

Butch licked his lips in anticipation of the reaction to the grim discovery of Gardner's body, which was now smashed to a pulp. *Well, whaddya know? I'm back to square one. Back at the scene of the crime with cops swarming all over my house. Just like old times.* An unwelcome memory flashed into his mind of the middle-aged social worker with the kind face who'd removed him from the scene following his father's murder of his mother. Butch could remember her grey curls and rosy complexion as clear as day. He even recalled the flowery scent on her neck as he'd clutched on to the collar of her patterned shirt as she carried him to safety, away from the crime scene and the inevitable swarm of police. The social worker had spoken to him softly in a soothing kindly tone as he tried to blank out the horror of what had just taken place. *No!* Butch shook his head vigorously. He could not afford to think Shaun's thoughts. He needed to think Butch's thoughts only.

As a pallid-faced Jock provided a detailed statement about the conversation that had taken place on the roof and the confession made by Butch, forensics got to work on the items in the black bin bag the young man had been waving around. The next job was to painstakingly go through his unit and the car port with a fine-tooth comb. The gruesome finding of Gardner's body under a pile of rubbish next to the skip next door was sickening. The anger and disgust towards Shaun Wallace was growing in intensity while he sat licking the burger remnants from the fingers on his free hand as though he didn't have a care in the world.

As Dylan observed his boss being discreetly carried off in a black body bag by men in white suits, he used all of his willpower not to lash out at Shaun Wallace. He leaned against the police van to steady himself and hoped no one noticed. Norris glanced his way and their eyes met. Neither of them had thought much of Gardner, but all the same he'd been killed in the line of duty and nothing could make a cop's blood boil more than to lose one of their own, especially when it was a meaningless death at the hands of a psychopath. They exchanged grim nods. A lengthy debriefing session would be required after what had already been the never-ending shift from hell.

CHAPTER 34

Given that Shaun Wallace cooperated and confessed to the murder of Paul and Jessica Henderson, Kate Jones and Detective Sergeant Robert Gardner, the police were a little more lenient when he was taken to the cells to be remanded into custody. Shaun was surprisingly lucid and agreed to remain compliant when questioned. Given his tendency to present as different personalities, the police hoped to strike while the iron was hot and have Shaun face court as soon as possible to give evidence. The wheels were in motion to seek legal representation for Shaun as well as have him undertake a mental health assessment. Dylan considered that he wouldn't be at all surprised if Shaun Wallace ended up being deemed unfit to stand trial, due to his poor mental health.

The following morning, the cell guard entered the cell due to Shaun not responding to prompts to get out of his bunk.

'Come on Wallace, get up! You don't want to make me come in there!'

Feeling furious with the young asshole who clearly thought he was above the rules, the cell guard stormed over to Shaun's bunk to give him the rocket up the ass he clearly needed. The cell guard prodded Shaun in the back and received no response. The stern-looking man frowned as the prisoner remained facing away from him. The cell guard rolled him over and sighed as he came face to face with Shaun's blank staring grey eyes. The cell guard felt for a pulse and confirmed he was well and truly dead. But nothing about the scene suggested Shaun had committed suicide or that anything untoward had happened. The post-mortem later revealed that structural abnormalities of the heart that had been present since birth had taken Shaun in his sleep.

There was no next of kin for Shaun and as such, the state government was responsible for arranging his cremation. Shaun's housing trust unit underwent a deep clean in preparation for the next young person on the waiting list for independent living accommodation. Within a matter of days, it was as though Shaun Wallace had never existed. The neighbours barely noticed his absence, given their permanently drug-affected state. The staff and young people at Woodies could not bring themselves to pay their respects to Shaun due to the enormity of the heinous crimes he'd committed. Their loyalty to Sarah came first and foremost. It was not lost on the myriad of professionals who'd either worked with or treated Shaun that his short life had been an extremely painful and tragic one. The general consensus reached was that he was now at peace and no longer tormented by his extreme trauma history.

As the news of Shaun Wallace's death become widely known, it received mixed reactions. Sandra Jones appeared nonchalant about it, which only reinforced to the police that she'd never really been invested in the wellbeing of her daughter Kate after all.

Sarah, Nick and Jean were grateful that there would not be a trial and were relieved the risk had been eliminated, now that Shaun was no longer a threat to their family. Sarah didn't feel she'd been denied the opportunity for revenge. She knew Shaun's whole life had felt like a punishment to him. Sarah hoped Shaun was now free from suffering, despite the pain he'd caused her.

Jock experienced mixed feelings about the whole thing. He still couldn't believe he'd successfully talked Shaun, aka Butch, into coming down from the roof and got him to agree to spare Sarah's life. Like Sarah, Jock hoped Shaun was now at peace, given how troubled he'd been throughout his short life. He debriefed with his beautiful wife Kellie and counted his blessings.

Gardner's ex-wife and daughter were seriously angry. They'd wanted to see the killer go to trial and serve a life sentence. Now he'd got off scot free by dying on them. They both felt a little guilty that they hadn't done more to help Gardner fight his demons while he was still alive, and so Angela stopped gossiping about her ex-husband and his sex addiction remained widely unknown. SA Police promised the family that they would pay a tribute to Gardner by lining the streets as a sign of respect on the day of his funeral.

Dylan and his team were relieved that the pressure was off. The murder cases had been solved and that was their main priority. They wouldn't be giving Shaun Wallace too much further thought, given that two new murder cases had come their way. When Dylan arrived home and shared the news of the imminent closure of the murder cases with Marie, she gave him a massive bear hug and snuggled into his chest. Marie looked up at her husband, the pride in her shining eyes evident as her words came out in a rush.

'I'm so proud of you for the work you do, Dylan. I don't think I tell you enough. I watched the news coverage and it must have been a really hellish job to attend when that kid was up on the roof with those poor people that used to care for him. I was so worried for your safety, you know! I realise we have been getting on each other's nerves lately but I'd be so lost if anything happened to you! I wasn't a fan of Gardner, but no one deserves to go like that. Angela and Maddison are beside themselves. I'm going to visit them tomorrow.'

Marie finally paused for a breath, her eyes glistening with tears. Dylan ruffled her hair and kissed the top of her head. He generally felt awkward on the rare occasions his wife lavished him with compliments and affection. Dylan gave his best appreciative smile, but as usual his words tumbled out sounding all wrong. 'That's a lovely thing to say my love. Have you been taking happy pills?'

Marie pulled away from him and scowled. 'Don't spoil a nice moment by being a smart ass! I was trying to show a bit of appreciation and don't need any snide remarks from you!'

Dylan raised his hands up in defeat. 'Whoa, you can't take a joke anymore. I'm just winding you up, my love!'

Marie pursed her lips and peered at him. She couldn't quite decide whether to place him in her bad books again or let him off the hook. She decided on the latter. Her husband wasn't to know his comment had hit a nerve. Marie had been at her GP that afternoon and been described anti-depressants to get her through menopause. When she'd listed all the ways that insomnia, brain fog and hot flushes were making her feel like a raving lunatic, the young Doctor Zhang had quickly prepared a prescription to help the wild-eyed middle-aged woman on her merry way.

Marie gave a weak smile. 'I've made a chicken risotto and there is a bottle of Rockford Alicante rosé in the fridge. How does that sound?'

Dylan gave a sigh of relief that she'd calmed down. 'Sounds perfect, honey. Just let me go and change.'

As Dylan undressed, he noticed a package on the chair in the corner of their bedroom. He picked it up and peered inside the plastic postage bag. The contents appeared to be lacy underwear. Dylan gasped with anticipation and delight. Maybe things were looking up on both the work and home front. Dylan rubbed his hands together with glee, then gathered up his dirty washing to take through to the laundry. This was definitely *not* the time to get on the wrong side of his wife.

EPILOGUE

April 2022

Following the death of Detective Senior Sergeant Robert Gardner, Dylan was now reporting to Detective Senior Sergeant Leonard Smythe, who appeared to be much easier going than his predecessor. Smythe signalled to Dylan to come into his office. As Dylan approached the office door, he felt the familiar dread associated with his previous meetings with Gardner.

Dylan was pleasantly surprised when Smythe waved a document at him with a grin on his face as he gestured for him to take a seat at the other side of his mahogany desk.

'The Superintendent is checking up on our wellbeing again so if you need to get things off your chest, let me know and I can get you booked in for a session with the Employee Assistance Program.'

Dylan shook his head. 'I think I'm good, boss. The team has been great at checking in with each other, albeit over one too many beers!'

Smythe gave a wry smile. 'I will pretend I didn't hear that you guys seek comfort from alcohol instead of the in-house quacks!' He laughed at his own joke. 'All jokes aside, you have way too much annual leave banked up. Is there any chance you want to schedule in time off so we can get your leave entitlements used up? Well actually, that's a rhetorical question because it's more of an order than a query.'

Dylan grinned at his new boss, his eyebrows raised in surprise. 'Well, that has to be the most pleasant order I've had in a while! I don't think I've had any time off in ages, now that I think of it!'

Smythe gave a curt nod. 'I'm all about making sure my team get equal work, rest and play. You are a diligent detective and I can see the past few weeks have taken their toll on you. There is no one on the team booked in for leave if you want to take the next couple of weeks off.'

While it had not even remotely crossed Dylan's mind to take time off, now that the offer was there, it suddenly sounded heavenly. He decided to snap up the opportunity in case Smythe changed his mind.

'Thanks, boss. I will apply for the leave straightaway.' Dylan felt lighter as he returned to his desk. Gardner had always been difficult about letting him take time off when he wanted to and it had been a bone of contention between him and his long-suffering wife. Dylan rang Marie immediately. Marie answered her mobile phone with her usual abrupt tone, expecting Dylan to warn her he would not be home until late, yet again. She was pleasantly surprised to hear a level of excitement in his voice. *Just like the old days.*

'Marie, the boss has just encouraged me to take the next couple of weeks off. Can you believe it? What's the chances of you getting leave too? We could take that trip to the Sunshine Coast at long last.'

Marie almost dropped her mobile phone in shock. She could not remember the last time she'd heard Dylan sound this enthused about anything and it was immediately infectious. Suddenly it occurred to Marie that her colleague Sandra had recently cancelled her annual leave until there was a little more certainty about traveling during the COVID-19 pandemic. This meant it was highly probable she would be allowed to take off the same two weeks as her husband, for once.

'That's a wonderful surprise, Dylan! Let me speak to my supervisor and I will get back to you ASAP! We can chat tonight. Okay, gotta go. Love you – bye!'

Dylan grinned. 'Love you too!'

Senior Constable Ben Norris returned to Victor Harbor police station when his secondment to the CIB team at Holden Hill police station came to an end. Ben somehow found himself on the same team as Constable Leanne Evans once again and started to wonder if fate had played a part in their reunion. He'd missed her company and the way she'd looked up at him with those sparkling aqua eyes when he took the lead in the more harrowing jobs they'd been to.

A few weeks later, Leanne realised over yet another round of after-work drinks that her ongoing debriefing sessions with Ben at the pub were now just an excuse to meet up. Their chemistry was becoming hard to deny, despite the professionalism they'd shown the whole time they'd been paired up at work. After his third beer, Ben finally summoned up the courage to reach over the table and take Leanne's hand in his own. Given that she didn't resist, he finally came out with it.

'It's time I told you how I feel about you.' Ben paused, eager to assess her reaction.

Leanne grinned back at him. 'If it makes your little speech any easier, I think you already know I feel the same way about you too!'

Ben beamed back at her, his grin widening by the second. 'What is it they say about love brewing in intense circumstances?'

Leanne slapped his hand playfully. 'That sounds like a line from a cheesy cop movie!'

Ben laughed. 'In all seriousness, though, I think we should keep it on the down-low until we see how things work out between us.

But… if we do end up being together, well … it wouldn't be too smart to keep working together. I guess it's a bit unethical too. Maybe we should be on different teams?'

Leanne nodded in agreement. 'Well, about that… maybe what I'm about to say next will make things a little easier in that regard.'

Ben looked intrigued as Leanne explained further. 'Okay, don't judge me, but I've decided to leave the police force. I've learned so much in a short time and gained great life skills but I just don't think I have the stomach to do this long term and deal with all the stuff we see. I get too upset. Those Port Elliot murders got to me more than I've been letting on and let's just say that time hasn't been a healer.'

Leanne lowered her eyes expecting either criticism or a lecture about why she should not give up and throw away a good career. Her dad had been on her back about quitting so soon and she was regretting telling him her thoughts, but she'd already made up her mind after speaking with a counsellor at the Employee Assistance Program. She wasn't going to budge, regardless of what anyone thought.

Leanne was surprised to note that Ben seemed relieved. 'I think that's really insightful of you to take ownership of how you feel. It's really brave to own it and walk away from a job that doesn't bring you joy. Well done, you! If I'm honest, I have been concerned at times by how consumed you've become at certain jobs, especially the Port Elliot murders. I know it's hard for any of us to switch off, but you in particular are a real worrier. I could see that right from the start.'

Leanne jumped off the bar stool and walked around the table to hug Ben. 'If you are trying to get off to the right start with me then you are doing a good job!'

Leanne buried her face in Ben's neck and inhaled the seductive woody fragrance of his aftershave. She hadn't figured out what her new career would be, but for now she was happy with her new man.

all the drama, he was long overdue a trip land. The cheeky Scotsman couldn't wait to d accumulated over the past year to depict his stralia. Nothing could compare to acting out n, knowing that his family and friends would tion at his hilarious take on things. Feeling of the trip, Kellie organised a FaceTime video Sandy, and his sister, Carol. Kellie adored her wait to see them again.

led to become one of the Richardson clan, nt simple yet beautiful garden wedding that over from Scotland for. Kellie laughed as she thought back to when the family had been staying with them in their Mount Barker home in the lead up to their big day. They'd shared many glasses of local wines and plenty of laughs. *The hills were certainly alive with the sound of music then!*

The family chatted excitedly on FaceTime for over an hour, planning all the things they'd do together when Jock and Kellie made the trip over to Scotland, once everything opened up post-COVID-19. They knew it might be a while off but it was good to have dreams to keep them all going. Just before the call ended, Jock cut in.

'Oh Mum, by the way, I meant to tell ye, I've been nominated for a bravery award, but like its nae big deal, eh?'

Sandy shrieked. 'What! That's amazing, son! Trust you tae play it down! You saved Sarah's life and we are all so proud o' ye!'

Carol nodded her head vigorously. 'I'm really proud of you, bro; that's amazing and well deserved.'

Jock was his usual humble and bashful self and played it down. 'Ah well, ye know me. I wis just trying tae help, like I always do.'

As the call ended and Jock poured himself a cider, he smiled to himself, secretly feeling pleased that he'd made his wife and family back home so proud.

Jock attempted to prepare Kellie for the trip to Scotland, even though they'd no idea when it could feasibly happen. He decided to teach his wife a bit of Scottish slang, given that she hadn't quite grasped it during their last visit there. He'd already taught her a fair bit but she needed more practice with various aspects of the pronunciation. The practice sessions often ended up with the pair of them rolling around in fits of laughter.

'Okay Kel, here is a test for ye. Let's say we are at my maw's hoose or ma sister's hoose and I want to say to you in Scottish lingo that I'd also like a beer, as in "I will have one too". What would I say?'

Kellie giggled, her blue eyes sparkling adoringly at her husband. She cocked her head to one side as she thought carefully about the pronunciation.

Jock nudged her playfully. 'Well c'mon then, blondie, what wid ye say?'

Without missing a beat Kellie blurted out, 'I'd say "I'll hae yin anaw, hen!'

Jock burst into applause, the adoration of his wife evident. 'Gid job! Ye are gonnae sound jist like the locals this time around, hen!'

The Easter period was fast approaching, which meant that the first anniversary of Paul and Jessica's death was imminent. Sarah was afraid to broach the subject with her mum, given that they'd gone away as a family at Easter for as long as she could remember. This year would look totally different and it made her feel incredibly sad.

Sarah took a deep breath and called Jean. 'Hi Mum, how are you today?'

Sarah heard a faint sigh at the other end. 'Sarah, my love, I think I know what you want to discuss. We always did have a psychic bond, didn't we?'

Sarah smiled. 'I can't deny that, Mama bear. So, about Easter?'

Jean inhaled as she pondered her reply. 'Sarah, I think we should go to Port Elliot as usual; we can't let the horror of the last year take over the rest of our lives. It's what Dad and Jess would want. Obviously, we will stay as far away from the last rental house as possible. If you agree, I think I'm ready to scatter Dad and Jessica's ashes at Middleton Beach.'

Sarah paused. She knew her mum was silently crying at the other end. 'I think that sounds perfect, Mum. The fresh air will do me good, especially with this blessed morning sickness I'm having at the moment.'

Jean perked up. 'What! My baby is pregnant again?'

Sarah smiled. 'Yes, Mum. I was going to tell you tonight over dinner but given the context of our conversation it just seemed really fitting to tell you now.'

Jean sobbed happy tears at the other end. 'I'm so happy, sweetie. That's the best news ever! Oh, and Sarah?'

'Yes, Mum?'

'I want you to know I have really turned a corner, love. I want you to stop worrying about me so much, okay? We will never ever get over what happened, but Dad and Jess would hate us to live the rest of our lives in misery. They'd want us to spend the Easter weekend in Port Elliot drinking wine and munching chocolate eggs as usual. Agreed?'

Sarah sagged with relief at Jean's words. 'I agree one hundred percent. I love you, Mum.'

Jean smiled. 'I love you too, sweetie. Now let's get this trip organised because we have left it a little late! I'm thinking maybe the Middleton Beach Huts for something a little different, if they still have any vacancies left for Easter?'

Sarah felt a huge weight lift from her shoulders. 'That sounds perfect, Mum. Let me know how you get on with booking and tell us if you need any help, okay?'

Jean's voice took on an excited tone. 'I'm onto it! Bye, love!'

Sarah and Nick could not thank Jock enough for having saved Sarah's life and they'd insisted on treating him and Kellie to a slap-up meal and a stay in a posh hotel, and lavished the pair with various gifts. During their last lunch catch-up Jock told them off.

'Look, guys, please nae mare gifts! Ye dinnae need tae thank me; I jist did what any decent guy wid do!'

The others exchanged a look, knowing most people would definitely not be brave enough to climb onto a roof to talk down a mentally unwell youth in a bid to save their friend's life. Jock was merely being his humble self. Sarah and Nick reflected on what Jock had said. They knew the couple well enough to realise that they were not flashy people and that perhaps their ongoing gifts were overwhelming for them. Sarah just wanted to show her gratitude and didn't know any other way to do so. Finally, Sarah and Nick came up with another way to honour their best friends.

Following a barbeque at Sarah and Nick's place, Sarah tapped her wine glass with a spoon to get everyone's attention.

'Jock and Kellie, we will stop buying you gifts to thank you if you will do us the honour of being the proud godparents of baby number two?'

Jock and Kellie exchanged amused smiles; they'd been content without children in their lives so far.

Jock spoke up. 'Aye hen, we can dae that but only if there's nae changing nappies and nae babysitting involved!'

Sarah burst out laughing, knowing he probably wasn't joking. 'So, what *would* you be prepared to do for our child in the capacity of the godparent role, then?' Sarah wiped away her tears of laughter as she waited with bated breath for Jock's response.

Jock thought about it for a few seconds. 'I'd teach them how tae camp, how tae mountain bike and how tae dae the gardening like a pro! Take it or leave it!' He gave a cheeky chuckle.

Sarah looked at Kellie, a sheepish grin lighting up her dainty features. 'Sorry, I should maybe let you guys have time to think about it instead of putting you on the spot like that! Seriously, no offence taken if you aren't keen on the whole godparent thing!'

Kellie laughed. 'We will do it, but the rules are what he said.' She pointed at her handsome husband.

Jock interjected. 'Oh, there's one more thing, hen! If it's a lassie, ye huv tae call her Jeannie after ma favourite song!'

Jock was joking, but Sarah and Nick were never too sure. The couple exchanged a doubtful glance. With that, Jock burst into song, grabbing a wooden spoon from the salad bowl to use as a guitar. Finn wandered over from his cubby house and watched his 'uncle Jock' in awe, his eyes round with amusement.

Jock stood on a chair and began to sing, as he took in the smiling faces all around him.

'A fine wee lass, a bonnie wee lass,
Is bonnie wee Jeannie McColl;
I gave her my mother's engagement ring
And a bonnie wee tartan shawl.
I met her at a waddin'
In the Co-operative Hall
I wis the best man
And she was the belle of the ball'

Everyone clapped and whistled and Jock took a bow.

Sarah would never have believed that she'd feel this happy and fulfilled again. She and Nick hadn't shared the news that they were expecting a girl, as they wanted to surprise the grandparents. As much as Sarah knew Jock was only teasing about the baby's name, it suddenly dawned on her that given her mum's name was Jean and therefore a shorter version of Jeannie, maybe they should consider this for their daughter's name after all. The idea hadn't even occurred to her before now. Sarah's mum would love that. *Thanks Jock, nice one!* As she looked on at her husband and best friends feeling full of joy, she patted her swollen belly and whispered, 'It's all going to be okay, little one.'

ACKNOWLEDGEMENTS

Thank you to all the readers who have taken a chance on me thus far and continued to follow my author journey up to now. It's surreal to believe that *Primed for Vengeance* is my fourth novel!

Like many other authors, I have days when I feel I can achieve anything and others where I feel like the biggest fraud! Thankfully the numerous writer friends I've accumulated along the way continue to remind me how unique and vulnerable we are to fly solo and put our imaginations out into the world for all to critique.

As can be said for many other types of creative artists, novel writing is often not all that lucrative (note that I still work full time too!) Authors are unique in the sense that a) people can borrow your books from the library for free; and b) if people read a good book, they tend to pass it on to their friend for free (and then they do the same, and so on). I do it myself! If I read a great book, I don't suggest that my friends buy the book, I just pass on my copy to them – we all do this, right?

So that means for every five or so readers, maybe only one of them purchased it. My point is that I write these novels for the love of it! It would be great to make lots of $$ but the one thing that ***anyone*** can do to help me out ***for free*** is to review my work on the following sites:

Amazon https://www.amazon.com/Gill-D-Anderson
Goodreads https://www.goodreads.com/author/show/19027510.Gill_D_Anderson

BookBub https://www.bookbub.com/authors/gill-d-anderson
Inhouse bookstore page https://inhousebookstore.com.au

Reviews can be terrifying! But they are crucial. So, when you see authors asking for them, try to help them out if you can. It's not about stroking their ego; it's about reinforcing to others that their work is worth reading (or not). This helps other readers decide if they should take a chance on an author. You wouldn't stay in a hotel that had no reviews, right? Well, books are no different. Writers need reviews to survive. There are over two million books published per year. I'm a teeny little fish in a big sea! So, to everyone who has read and reviewed my novels (I read every single one), you honestly have given me the best possible gift of all and I thank you from the bottom of my heart. Please follow me on the following sites:

Facebook (Gill D Anderson author) https://www.facebook.com/contemporary.adult.fiction
Instagram (gillyanderson71) www.instagram.com>gillyanderson71
Twitter https://twitter.com/gilliananders16

Feel free to share my posts, invite people to like my social media pages and spread a little kindness along the way.

I'd like to thank my husband, who is one in a million and a total saint for not complaining during the periods where I spend half my life at the keyboard. During this time, he brings me endless coffee and does more than his fair share of the chores without whinging! I love you with all my heart, Brent xx

Last but not least, I'd like to thank Jacki F and the fabulous team at InHouse Publishing for their wonderful service, professional advice and their collective wisdom. My novels can be purchased from their bookstore in Queensland using the following link:

https://inhousebookstore.com.au/search?q=gill+d+anderson

Printed in Great Britain
by Amazon

64979586R00135